Infatuation

E. Hughes

Copyright © 2008 E. Hughes

Publisher: Love-LovePublishing
P.O. BOX 258136 Madison, WI 53725
ISBN: 978-0-9973200-7-7
Library of Congress Control Number: 2018902353
Title: Infatuation/ E. Hughes
Digital distribution I Love-LovePublishing, 2017
Paperback I Love-LovePublishing, 2017

Other novels by this author:

Business as Usual
Disappear, Love
The Chronicles of Sapphire (as Sophie Lace)
A Mediterranean Romance: The Capa Royals
Beyond the Plain
Hello

To my friends and family: Thank you for the
endless feedback and encouragement…
With love, -E

INTRODUCTION

Georgine Louvelle looked up, bright stage light beaming directly into her eyes. Renard, the actor at *Le Caniche Rose*, whom she had met earlier that night and was very much attracted to, hovered above her and knelt...moving the light around his shadowy figure as a handsome American stranger seated in the front row, patiently observed from behind with a worried look on his face. Renard was a sight for sore eyes.

"Are you okay, Chéri?" he whispered. His lips were a breath away from her face as he maneuvered her away from the floor. Georgie sat up, resting in the nook of his open arms. His hand was warm against her spine.

It took a moment for Paris and the burlesque to come flooding back... she was supposed to pose nude in the tableau vivant, then blackness...

"*Where am I?*" Georgie grumbled.
"You fainted," Renard replied.

Her lashes fluttered, as fractured memories of her arrival in Paris slowly filtered into her brain…everything *except* what happened before the black curtain fell….

CHAPTER ONE

After one disappointing audition after another it was a dream come true when Lucky called to tell his single most important client (*his only client*), the good news... that she had been cast to star in a French stage play on Pigalle's 18th Arrondissement near the *real* Moulin Rouge.

With only her mother's blessing, Georgine Louvelle hopped on a plane to Paris with hopes of a starring role in the show. *Hell, Josephine Baker was huge in France, so why not?*

The café, *Le Caniche Rose*, was in Paris' Red Light district where *"courtesans"* lurked on sidewalks and seedy sex shops decorated street corners. Huge signs written in English displayed impolite words in big bright lights; "Pussy! Sex! Fuck! SEX SEX SEX!"

The buildings weren't tall and grand with the Eiffel Tower lighting the background like on all the post cards she'd seen of Paris in hospital gift shops and airports... they were small century-old whitewashed stone buildings stacked side to side like blocks of Lego with built in flashing neon signs — some of them with broken bulbs.

The café, she was told, was in a dark alleyway between two closely situated apartment buildings, had sounded sketchier and sketchier by the minute. Bracing herself for the worse, Georgine clutched her suitcases, designer bags, and deftly avoided the drunkards, beggars and tramps on the sidewalk...some of whom pushed and shoved in desperation, trying to scalp tickets to Moulin Rouge, the most famous show in the 18th Arrondissement.

Georgie promised to strangle Lucky the second she laid her eyes on him for sending her to Paris in the first place. She wondered if she could trust him. She had only known the man a few weeks when he offered her what she thought was the opportunity of a lifetime.

But never one to shy away from danger, Georgie had always been intrigued by the dark side of life. A side, she'd only glimpsed through fractured memories she'd never fully been able to piece together. A side, her parents had taken great care to protect her from. For better or worse, she was a prisoner of her own mind and had always fantasized that if she couldn't find her way back to the past, the past would eventually find her. There was something dark and shifty about Lucky...something that piqued her curiosity. Something that demanded, or hinted at clues to a past forgotten. Across the world, in another country she could finally escape her family's grip... Lucky had merely been a means of escape. She was finally free!

A few days after their first meeting he sent her audition tape to a producer in France and not long after, the man called to tell her she had gotten the part.

Bustling with excitement, Georgie drove to her parent's house all the way in Connecticut to tell them the good news.

"Who is he and where did he come from?" her father asked. "Out of all the starving actresses in New York, he picked you?"
Louis Louvelle called the low rent talent agent a greasy door to door salesman and warned her not to go.

Why didn't I listen to him? Why am I so hard headed?" she thought.

Georgie followed directions on a map Lucky had given her to an alleyway. Enveloped by sudden darkness and a draft that swept from the shaft at the top of the building to the ground, sweeping her hair into a frenzy, Georgie contemplated backing out until she noticed a neon sign bearing the words *"Le Caniche Rose"* blinking above the door of an underground café. She looked at the sheet in her hand. The addresses matched.

Joie de vivre!

Georgie's dream had finally come true. She was in Paris, city of lights...mere steps from her new career at *Le Caniche Rose*. There, ambient sounds battled it out. A mellow tune wafting out of the underground café intermingled with the pots and pans clanging sound of jazz playing in a nearby apartment building. She tapped her feet as looked up, taking in the height of the towering Euro-ghetto apartment building.

Bursting with excitement, Georgie hurried down the basement stairs and stood outside of the café. She read the handwritten sign on the window:

"Ouvrez pour des affaire."

Only, *Le Caniche Rose (The Pink Poodle)*, wasn't open for business yet. It was dark as dusk inside. She took a deep breath and knocked on the door anyway, eager to greet her new boss. A husky, grim-looking man in a blonde Marilyn Monroe wig opened the door.

"Ah! La femme la American! Où étiez-vous ? Vous nous avez rendus en retard! Quel est votre no?"

"Georgine...but my friends call me Georgie."

She smiled and extended a hand but the man waved her off.

"No! En Francais. Nous parlons seulement français dedans ici!"

"—Sorry. I mean, Pardonnez-moi. Bonjour. Je m'appelle Georgine."

"Oui, Oui, come inside, your French is not very good."

"Neither is your English, but you don't see

me complaining."

The man rolled his eyes.

"Come, meet your new colleagues. My name is Joe."

He said it with an affected American accent. She could tell Joe was not his real name.

Georgine followed him inside and looked around the dimly-lit underground cafe. Beyond a well stocked bar, a kitchen and twenty or so tables, was a room where a crowd of men dressed in various attire gathered around a roulette table. Topless women, some with tassels swinging from their brassieres walked around with drinks on little trays in the smoke-filled room. Waifs, alcoholics, and a few unseemly looking patrons occupied the tables, some of them nodding in and out of sleep like they could care less about the stage or anything else in the room. What in the hell was this place? *'Was any of this even legal?'* Georgie wondered.

Behind her, the door suddenly banged open, and in walked a man with the biggest nose she had ever seen. He stopped, looked her up and down and grumbled, "Get the fuck out of the way," before finding a poker game to play at a nearby table. She tried not to look startled as he staggered by, swirling the drink in his hand before gulping it down in one swig. Georgie was about five seconds from giving the crude Frenchman a piece of her mind, but lost her train of thought as a horde of circus clowns in a rainbow of curly neon wigs ran by, one of them stopping to honk the boobs of a topless waitress, who promptly tossed a drink in his face. The café was in utter chaos.

"Don't worry, they are almost finished," Joe whispered, waving a topless waitress over to them for a drink.

Georgie followed Joe's line of view to the stage where she saw him; a vision of loveliness amid the chaos. Posing naked among a group of actors before a cardboard background depicting a serene life-sized impressionist work of art, that might have been painted by a wannabe Monet, stood *Renard*. She watched, mesmerized by the stage as the handsome actor engaged in a mouth to mouth kiss with one of the other performers, a man who looked to be a few years younger. The red curtain dropped to sparse inattentive applause, and the actors dispersed, some going backstage, others coming down the side steps, heading towards the bar where Georgie waited with Joe.

Renard was among the group. He smiled as he walked towards them, and she damn-near blushed, trying her best not to stare at his well defined chest, muscular stomach, and everything else on display.

"We are not busy. As you can see, we have only a few customers inside."

Georgie nodded and feigned a smile at Joe as the group approached, all of them curious to meet the new face of the café.

"I'm Georgine, nice to meet you. What exactly, is *this*?" she asked, gesturing toward the stage.

"We were performing le *tableau vivant*... I'm Renard," the handsomest man in the room, replied.

He was dark haired with a smile that could raise the dead. The stubble on his face lent him an air of masculinity, a strong contrast to his heavy lids and feminine dark eyelashes. He flashed a smile, showing a mouth full of straight white teeth.

"A tableau vivant? That means, "'*Living painting,' right*?"

"Yes, *yes*...something like that." He studied her face, as if to take in every detail of her rich mocha-complexion and soft, pillowy lips.

"Well, it's a pleasure to meet you, Renard."

"The pleasure is all mine, *Miss* Louvelle."

Renard kissed the back of Georgie's hand, lifting his dark eyes to meet hers as his lips pressed against her well-manicured fingers. The last thing Georgie wanted was some naked stranger's wet lips on her skin. She glared as she quickly snatched her hand away, wiping the moisture away with a napkin from the bar. Renard smiled, shrugging his muscular shoulders. She tried to keep her eyes on his face, anything not to look down.

"We need *Va-va voom* for *Le Caniche Rose*. With the sexy shows and Moulin Rouge just down the street, business is slow," Joe said.

"So where's the rest of the cast?"

She tipped to the side and stole a look at the stage again. It didn't seem to her —large enough to support the cast in the script Lucky had given her. There was a red curtain and a wide oblong shaped platform surrounded by tables on each side and not much stage.

"When do rehearsals begin? When is opening night?" Georgie asked.

"What you mean 'opening night?' You start today."

She gave him a stupid look. "Are we adlibbing our lines? I don't understand…"

"What lines?"

"The lines in your script."

"There is no script. You will undress for le *tableau vivant*."

Georgie shook her head in disagreement then opened her shoulder bag to give Joe a copy of the stage play Lucky had given her. He flipped through the pages.

"Lucky said you watched my video."

Joe sucked the filter of his cigar deeply then turned the page. "Yeah. So?"

"He said you watched my audition. You

offered me the lead in your play." She looked around, seeing only a dimly lit dump. "Am I in the right place?"

Joe gave a phlegmatic cough and belched out a laugh. "A stage play! I hire you to do burlesque for the tableau vivant. What do you mean, *stage play*? There's no playing on our stages...."

Georgie nearly choked on Joe's cigar fumes, fanning smoke away from her face as she shook her head. Did he say, *burlesque?*

Suddenly it all made sense. The Red Light District, the seamy underground café, the "VIP" rooms and topless women roaming around the back with drinks on their trays...

Georgie snatched the script out of Joe's grubby hands.

"A burlesque show? I beg your pardon but I am a trained actress and dancer!" she shrieked. "I didn't travel halfway across the world to strip in a damned *titty* bar."

"Lucky told me you are a famous burlesque actress. You make *Le Caniche Rose* sexy, like Broadway 'eh? You are our big American star!"

Georgie shrugged away from Joe's hand, which came to a rest on her shoulder.

"You don't understand... I worked on Broadway before but I'm not a burlesque dancer," she pleaded.

Joe rolled his eyes. "I don't care what you are, get undressed and make a good show for me."

"I didn't come here to star in a burlesque. I was cast in a stage play. So get it through your thick head! I'm not doing it. You and your little minions coerced me into flying here under false pretenses! I want a ticket back to the States immediately or I'm reporting you to the embassy."

Georgie stuck her hand out and gestured for Joe to pay up.

"You no dance, I no pay. I pay a lot of money to get you here. What you think? This is a free vacation?"

"It's clearly a misunderstanding. I'm *not* a stripper."

"Misunderstanding or not, I won't pay another Euro until you perform. You could do worse. If we were Russian mobsters you would be beaten and forced into a prostitution ring. Be grateful all you have to do is dance."

"A p*rostitution* ring?"

She'd seen investigative news segments about it. Mobsters disguised as "modeling" recruiters luring pretty young girls across Europe with promises of making them international stars. Georgie stared at the man with wide eyes. She couldn't believe this was happening.

"Don't worry. I run an honest business. You'll get money to go home. But you must earn it first."

"Fine! Take me to my dressing room. I'll dance tonight, collect my money, and get the hell out of here first thing tomorrow."

"If you think you can earn the money in one night, eh, be my guest."

Joe shrugged and began to sweep the floor. Georgie was just about to tap him on the shoulder to give him a piece of her mind when Renard tugged at her elbow. She turned to face him and walked into another cloud of smoke, coughing as he drew from the filter of his cigarette, blowing a perfect ring of smoke toward her face.

"We'll combine elements of tableau vivant and burlesque. Joe has the right idea for once, don't you think? Besides, it doesn't hurt that we get to look at you."

"I'm not exactly pleased with the arrangement so spare me the small talk..." Georgie hotly replied, sliding the script back into her shoulder bag.

"Is something wrong?" Renard asked.

"-Mademoiselle!"

Before Georgie could fathom a reply, Joe approached her from behind. She turned, eyes glaring as he handed her a skimpy pink bustier with matching gloves and leotard. The ensemble included tacky cone shaped cups to cover her breasts like the ones Madonna wore in her *Vogue* music video.

Georgie held the skimpy garment with the tip of her thumb and index finger as though a great stink had risen from it.

Joe frowned.

"The suit has never been worn. Put it on."

Georgie sighed in exasperation as he turned on his heels and walked away. She had two options, which was to call her father and hear about it for the rest of her life, or deal with it like an adult and get out of the situation on her own... whether she had to go on stage or not. She didn't even have a hotel room. Leaving Joe's establishment meant finding and paying for a hotel suite she couldn't possibly afford. Renard pulled her aside.

"You were saying...?"

"I'm here for a role in a stage play. No one said anything about a burlesque show or posing nude in front of some painting."

Georgie sighed and tried not to weep as Renard put his hands on her shoulders.

"Take a deep breath. It's okay. We'll figure something out."

"It's not okay! I'm thoroughly pissed. They lied to me!" she hissed.

"I don't want you to be unhappy, Georgine. Forget Joe. You should fly home *immediately*."

"I would but I'm broke. I can't afford to buy a plane ticket."

"Don't worry about the ticket. I'll buy it for you myself on one condition..."

Georgie's heart lifted a little...

"Yes?"

"You spend the night with me."

Georgie groaned, angrily throwing her hands in the air.

"I'll pass. I've my share of slime balls for the night."

Renard staggered back, clutching his heart like he had been shot in the chest.

"Ouch! I didn't mean it like that! Forgive me, Cherie. My English isn't perfect. I meant, spend the night in Paris with *me*. I would never take advantage of your...*situation*," he offered smoothly.

Georgie gave him a dubious look. He gripped her shoulders again. Almost any excuse to touch her.

"I just want to show you Paris. The real Paris. This café is... unforgiveable."

Renard said it the way the French say it, "*Paireee.*" He looked sincere. Then she remembered the boy on boy kiss she'd seen between him and another actor on stage. She'd forgotten he was gay. With her thick shoulder length dark hair, perfect figure, almond shaped eyes and creamy mocha complexion, Georgie was used to being hit on. She felt foolish for even thinking Renard was interested.

"Apology accepted. I wish Joe would do the honorable thing and send me back."

"Asking Joe to act like a gentleman would be like asking a dog not to piss on a fire hydrant. The show wouldn't be right if you performed against your will."

Georgie nodded. They stood silently, gazing into each other's eyes until Renard's towel began to slip. He let her go, catching it before it crumpled to his feet.

"I know," Georgie acquiesced. "I appreciate the offer but I can't accept your money. I'll earn it on my own."

Renard broke into a smile.

"You'll earn enough money for a plane ticket in no time. Though I must admit, my motives for wanting you to stay are selfish… we have time to get to know each other."

"Assuming of course, I'm interested in getting to know you…"

"All in due time, Cherie."

Talking to Renard made her feel better. "Thank you," Georgie said.

She pulled him into a hug but Renard

quickly drew away, blushing as he adjusted the towel around his waist. The scruffy stubble on the side of his face brushed against Georgie's cheek. She liked the caress of his facial hair against her skin.

"Just one question…."

"What is it?"

"Why me? There are at least a dozen waitresses here who could do it."

"Yes, but none as talented or beautiful as you. Joe was excited to bring you here, he sings your praises, says you bring him a lot of money. Money is all that greedy pig ever thinks about."

"Money? From *me*? But I haven't done anything yet," she gasped.

Renard was just flattering her.

"Tell that to Joe."

"The plot thickens…" Georgie said, breaking into a smile.

"I'll take you to the dressing room. He wants you to start right away."

"Without a rehearsal? What am I supposed to do?"

"Look beautiful."

Renard led her to a dressing room where Georgie freshened up, did her makeup, and changed into the outfit Joe had given her. A few minutes later, she stood before a floor-length mirror and frowned, turning a full 360 degrees as she examined the ill-fitting suit.

The dressing room was small, packed with glittery costumes and a vanity. She sat down, ruminating over her decision to go on stage when someone knocked loudly on the door.

"Sortez ! Il est temps d'aller à l'étape," a course sounding voice yelled out.

Georgie braced herself, opened the door and walked out of the room on shaky legs.

The backstage area bustled with activity. Stage hands, actors and crew members hustled by at a fast pace, nearly knocking her into oblivion as they scurried by. She stumbled out of their path, almost pushing through the dark red stage curtain ahead of herself, her head poking through the curtain. Georgie surveyed the audience.

Seated at a table close to the stage was a handsome, sophisticated stranger in an expensive business suit. He sat disinterested, huffing on a cigar as he waited for the show to start. His manners were befitting a man of wealth, accustomed to getting attention as a pair of topless waitresses stood by, giggling and pointing in his direction. Georgie took a deep breath. The man looked up, and their eyes connected. Hazel brown orbs gazed into her dark brown eyes. She slipped behind the curtains again, overcome with an irrational feeling of having seen him before.

The room was thick with recreational smog.

The audience had grown considerably... just in time to see her make a fool of herself. *"Just get it over with and call home!"* a voice in her head whimpered.

Renard and the other actors filed out onto the stage. He signaled Georgie to join them. She went over the routine they discussed over and over again until the curtains opened. *Walk out and disrobe in front of the fountain.*

Renard and the others were already in place, posing with perfect stillness when Alphonso the piano player began to play.

"Get out there!" Joe shouted. "I'm not paying you to stand around."

Georgie opened the curtain and walked out.

It was the last thing she remembered before the lights in the room went black.

CHAPTER TWO

Georgie looked up, bright stage light beaming directly into her eyes. Renard hovered above her and knelt...moving the light around his shadowy figure as the handsome American stranger from the front row patiently observed from behind with a worried look on his face. Renard was a sight for sore eyes.

"Are you okay, Chéri?" he whispered. His lips were a breath away from her face as he maneuvered her away from the floor. Georgie sat up, resting in the nook of his open arms. His hand was warm against her spine.

It took a moment for Paris and the burlesque to come flooding back... she was supposed to pose nude in the tableau vivant, then blackness...

"*Where am I?*" Georgie grumbled.

"You passed out," Renard replied.

It wasn't the first time it happened. Sometimes she'd awake with little memory at all, hence, the disjointed memories plaguing the recesses of her mind. Georgie remembered pushing through a red stage curtain, but everything else was a blur.

Doctors had long given up on finding a cure for her inexplicable brain disorder. Anxiety and high stress situations caused her to blank out, resulting in permanent memory loss, and an inability to recall recent events. It was a rare, incurable form of anterograde amnesia. Georgie was used to performing in front of crowds in American stage plays, and the occasional small role on Broadway, but the stress of being alone in a foreign country, and the mysterious American in the front row had been too much. She remembered him...the man sitting next to the stage when she stuck her head through the curtain.

"Show us your tits!" he yelled, making the audience laugh after she finally came out. "You like money, don't you?" he sneered, as she gazed into the bright stage light, trying to get a better glimpse of his face. "Then please, Madam, show us your tits!"

Georgie was a New Yorker. She was used to

rude people and the hustle and bustle of life, so it wasn't his jeering that made her faint. Something else, something someone said had made her tremble...had made her feel inexplicably afraid. But once the black veil came crashing down on her consciousness, everything that happened out there disappeared. The only thing she recognized at that moment was the warmth in Renard's eyes, as fractured memories of their earlier conversation slowly filtered into her brain.

"What are you doing? Get up and take your clothes off," Joe griped, stampeding toward them like a rhinoceros.

"What happened?" Georgie grumbled.

"You fainted," Renard answered, as he walked a woozy Georgie backstage and ushered her toward a chair.

"You ruined my show. I should charge you for all the money I lost," Joe complained, from behind.

Georgie ignored the pushy old man and pushed to the wardrobe closet... slamming the door behind her. She could hear Joe ranting up a storm in French as she slipped out of her costume into a thick blue robe. When she came out a few minutes later, he was still waiting with pissed off look on his face.

Georgie tied the sash of the robe around her waist and fixed him with a nasty stare.

"Wha-what is this you do? This is a Burlesque. They want to see tits!"

"I'm not going out there again… not like this."

She gestured toward the orange leopard print leotard with the cone shape breast cups. Georgie wondered how the old man managed to convince her to put it on in the first place.

Joe shook his head, "If you not perform, what you come here for?"

Georgie folded her arms, kicked one of her long legs out of the robe she wore and threw her hip to the side.

"I don't know what Lucky told you, but I'm not a stripper and I'm not taking my clothes off. If you want me to stay, I'll choreograph something before I go out there again. And you will give me a room and a week to rehearse. Got it?"

Were it not for the fact that she was stuck in Paris having arrived with a one way ticket and no means of getting home she would have been on the next flight back to the States the moment she set her designer high heeled shoes on that dirty Pigalle Street sidewalk.

"After your terrible performance you are in no position to negotiate. However, I will be generous and give you a week to prepare. But I pay for performance only. I do not pay for dance rehearsal. Room and board will come out of your wages."

He went into his pocket and pulled out a ring of keys. He gave Georgie a key to apartment 7.

It was the first good thing that happened to her all day.

"Take the back stairs behind *the* bar up to *the* second floor."

Georgie followed Joe's instructions and slipped through the exit behind the bar. She walked up a flight of stairs to ground level from the café, which was in the basement of the apartment building... then walked another two flights to the second floor.

She considered, but only briefly as she walked to her room, asking her parents for money to get home. But the last thing she wanted to do was prove her father right or give him an excuse to rub the situation in her face. She could hear him already... *"I told you!"*

Louis Louvelle warned his daughter not to quit her job as a dance teacher at Cornwall Ballet School... but it was a dream come true when the opportunity to go to Paris fell into her lap. Who could blame her for taking it?

Georgie unlocked the door to apartment 7 and quickly stumbled inside with three suitcases. The apartment was not as bad as she expected it to be, only smaller. It was a sparsely furnished studio apartment. There was a sofa, a lamp, a coffee table, a changing area, and a bed. Surprisingly, noise from the basement was muted. There were even pots and dishes in the kitchen cabinets – but no food.

Georgie sighed and flopped down onto the thick sofa cushions, kicking her shoes off. She wiped the makeup from her face with the back of her hand. After a short rest and a good cry she got up and ripped the sheets off of her bed. She washed them by hand in the kitchen sink then hung them on the clothesline over the fire escape to dry.

Georgie stood on the balcony, inhaled the night air and marveled at her minor achievement. She suspected the sheets would dry in a matter of hours. A strong wind blew a flush of warm air into the alley.

CHAPTER THREE

The next day, Georgie woke with a start. Someone was knocking on the door. She wiped the sleep from her eyes and climbed out of bed. It was eight in the morning. She put her silk white and red kimono on, tied the sash around her waist and opened the door. Renard was on the other side. Waking up to Renard and his sexy bedroom eyes wasn't the worst thing that ever happened to her. *'That's for sure!'* she thought with a mental nod. He looked like he had stepped out of a Calvin Klein ad. His hair was wet like he was fresh out of the shower. He looked scrumptious in a plain white t-shirt and a pair of jeans. He rubbed his stomach, lifting his shirt a few inches. Her eyes followed a faint trail of stomach hair into the top of jeans.

"Renard? What are you doing here?"

Georgie put her hands on her hips and moved aside as Renard walked in. He sat a brown paper bag full of goods on her coffee table and replied to her in English.

"I'm sorry about what happened at the show yesterday. It was unfortunate."

"Not to make excuses but I was exhausted. I didn't know Joe expected me to jump into a routine straight out of the airport. I thought I was here for a part in a stage play."

"Joe is a greedy insensitive idiot. You are tired from your flight still? I brought coffee and scones if you're hungry."

Georgie smiled. She was starved! "You didn't have to do that…"

Renard shrugged his muscular shoulders.

"We all have to eat." He walked into the kitchen and brought plates back to the table.

"Smells good! Oh *Renard*…" she gushed. "How will I *ever* repay you?"

He looked at her, his eyes working their way up from her feet to the top of her dark head.

"I'm sure I'll think of something," he answered.

"How long have you worked at the Pink Poodle?"

She followed him with her eyes, staring at his sexy rump as he walked to a chair and sat down.

"About a year and a half."

"The other guys?"

"We start together. Why you come all the way from America to work in this dump? They don't have dumps in America?"

Georgie laughed and Renard flashed her his million dollar smile... Georgie passed him a scone.

"I thought I was going to a beautiful classy place... like *Moulin Rouge*. I had no idea the place was literally, a hole in a wall."

"The Moulin Rouge!" Le Moulin Rouge? Ce n'est pas un endroit elegant!"

"It's not?"

"Georgine... There are beautiful women in Moulin Rouge but the Red Light District is a crummy part of Paris. You see? Lot of tough guys here. A lot of women and prostitutes. Money, money, money!"

The scone he put in his mouth made a lump in his cheek.

"As soon as I can afford it I'm going home."

Renard gave her a shocked look. "Home? Already? But you haven't seen Paris...the real Paris. *Beautiful* Paris..."

Georgie sat on the sofa. "Oh, I've seen enough! I assure you…"

"But this is only a small part of France… I love this city, this country. One day I will give you a tour. What do you want to see? The Eiffel Tower?"

"Maybe," she smiled, a wink in her eyes.

"You ever visit Paris before?"

"To see my grandparents. But that was a long time ago… I'd love another tour of France."

She blew the surface of the coffee he gave her and took a sip.

"If you stay longer I'll take you in August for holiday. How does that sound?"

"Is this an actual date?"

"Does it sound like a real date?"

Georgie gave him a puzzled look. When she first arrived she'd seen him kissing another man on stage at the end of their performance. Was the boy on boy kissing just an act? Or an act of attraction?

"I'm surprised you're interested in taking me anywhere. Aren't you gay?"

Renard gave her a look of mock surprise.

"Gay! Je ne suis pas un homosexuel!"

He moved from the chair he sat in and sat beside her on the sofa.

"Let me prove to you that I am a man…. Je veux te faire l'amour, Georgine."

Renard slipped a hand to her inner thigh and nuzzled the side of her neck softly and slowly trailing her flesh until he was kissing her lips. His mouth was soft, moist, and warm. She felt hot and tingly inside and out but pushed her arm forward to put some distance between them.

"You're so beautiful. I can't resist you," he whispered.

"Don't make excuses," Georgie said.

Renard smiled and covered her knees with the end of her robe, setting it back in place as he stood. She spun around in her seat and watched as he walked toward the door.

"Enjoy your scones."

And with that, he was gone.

Georgie paced the floor. It was all she could do to ignore heated thoughts of rolling around in bed with Renard. She could see him clear as day, right there on her pillow, tangled sheets in disarray around his naked body.

To distract herself, Georgie opened a window to cool her heated flesh and tried to think of a routine for the show... but to no avail. So she scrubbed the bathroom, swept the floors, cleaned the oven, styled her hair then borrowed a bike from Joe. She rode to the market wearing a sundress, a pair of sandals, and a locket with a picture of her parents inside.

She endured the hagglers and catcalls better than she did the first time as she made her way back to the apartment. By nightfall she finally had an idea for the show.

A week later Georgine was in full swing and doing her first Burlesque.

The first night was a blur as she stood on stage and touched her pouted lips to make sure she hadn't eaten the perfectly applied lipstick from her mouth. She heard a screeching noise and looked up. Joe pointed a lamp at the stage. The light was blinding. But that was a good thing. She couldn't see the audience and was grateful she didn't have to look at their faces.

Save for the stage light, the cafe was

smoky, dark, and hot. Drunkards were slumped over their tables and the shadows of courtesans in obvious acts of sexual activity with customers, flickered against the thin walls of the shoji screens separating the rest of the café from the VIP rooms.

Georgie cleared her throat and the microphone screeched in resistance. A few people looked up, disinterested looks in their eyes. She ignored Joe's annoyed facial expressions and flailing arms until he smacked a hand over his forehead in defeat, whispering in a hoarse voice for her to start.

So Georgie sang her song...thinking of home, her family's apple orchard, and how much she missed her friends in New York. She stood on the tiny Parisian stage, pouring her heart out, praying the crowd liked her song. When she was done, the audience was silent, and unbeknownst to Georgie, very much in awe. The applause that followed swelled as she left the stage.

She raced to her changing room where Renard met her with a hug. He spun her around.

"That was beautiful! You did it Georgine."

"You sure?"

She gave him a worried look.

"It was gorgeous…they love you," Renard assured her.

The look in his eyes spoke how much he loved her too. Renard lit one of his cigarettes and placed it between her lips. Georgie blew a puff of smoke in the air and watched as the cloud rose to the ceiling. She hated cigarettes but this was a victory smoke.

Joe was so pleased with Georgie's performance that he hired a seamstress to make new costumes in her size the very next day.

Georgine employed a different theme for her burlesque show every day of the week and two months later, the show was opening to sold out crowds.

With so much money on the line, Joe did what he could to keep Georgie from going home. He deducted over the top fees from her pay for room and board; charged her money for the material his seamstress used in the costumes, and added rental fees for the dressing room. It didn't matter that he was making a killing on the cover charge and drinks or the fact that someone was already paying him an exorbitant amount of money to keep Georgine Louvelle in Paris.

CHAPTER FOUR

"Go! Go out there and mingle."

It was a nightly complaint. Instead of mingling with the crowd after the show, visiting tables and flirting with men who "paid good money" to see her, Georgie went straight to her dressing room.

"You don't pay me enough to mingle."

"People pay money to see you and you won't even talk to them."

"They pay money to you. I don't get any of it so why should I care!"

Georgie slammed the dressing room door in Joe's face and slumped down in her chair. She rolled her eyes; tired of noise, smoke, and blabbering drunks when a knock on the door snapped her out of despair. She was just about to tell Joe off, thinking he was there to bother her about mingling again, but to her surprise, Renard was on the other side the door.

"Hey, beautiful."

He gave her a kiss on both sides of her face then strolled in, lighting the cigarette in his mouth.

"Hey babe, what's up?"

Georgie sat in front of the vanity and powdered her brown face.

"I'm going to my family's cottage in Brittany and I want you to go with me."

Georgie's smile was ear to ear. "Really?"

She was surprised that after only two months of going out with Renard that he wanted to show her off to his family. He was proud of her and what she did for Joe's café. But Georgie was less confident about her role… going from actress to Burlesque dancer wasn't exactly the most accomplished thing she had ever done. All she wanted was enough money to get back home but the two of them barely earned enough to pay the bills.

"I told them about you and they can't wait to meet you in person."

"For holiday?"

"Oui."

He took the cigarette out of his mouth and kissed her on the lips. He was a good man, a patient man. Despite the numerous times they made out but had yet to make love.

Meeting Renard's parents was a serious gesture. Her stomach was in knots.

"Are you sure? You don't think it's too soon?"

"I wouldn't ask if I wasn't sure. I love you. You should know that by now, yes?"

Renard held her hand and kissed her again and her arms instinctively moved to his neck as he squeezed her close.

"Sure, I'll go to Brittany with you."

"Good…"

He smiled then pulled out of her grasp. Someone was knocking on the door. Renard opened it and Joe came rushing inside.

"Georgie! Come with me. It's urgent!"

Georgie met him by the door. "What's wrong?" A desperate image of her parents was the first thing that popped into her head.

"You have a visitor."

She didn't know that many people in France. Just the guys, the waitresses, and Joe.

"Who is it? What do they want?"

"I know I promised never to ask you to entertain guests in the VIP room…"

"Hell no! Don't even think about it!" she interrupted, before he could get the words out of his mouth.

"He said he'll pay whatever you ask."

She was about five seconds from slapping Joe across his hairy face. "Do I look like a whore to you?"

"I assured him that you weren't that kind of girl. Georgie... come, you are my friend. This is good money. How can you turn it down? He paid 3,000 dollars to see you."

"To see me?"

"For a few minutes of your time, nothing more. Come on, Georgie...do it for me."

"Do it for you? Are you nuts? You can fire me if you want to but I'm not going out there and I'm not going to the VIP room."

The line had to be drawn somewhere.

"Fine! We lose a lot of money because of you."

"Deduct it from my paycheck like you always do."

"Don't tempt me!"

Joe stormed out and Renard slammed the door behind him.

"I should have left the two of you alone. If you wish to go, do not delay on my account."

"I didn't say no because of you. I said no because I'm not that kind of girl. I'm offended he would even ask."

A knock on the door again made Georgie look around. Joe pushed the door open and walked inside.

"He said he will give me an additional 3,000 dollars. And if you don't talk to him, he will take his money back and leave. He said he's not interested in the other girls. He wants you."

"If I go out there then what's in it for me?"

"I'll give you half."

"Half?"

Half was more than enough to buy a ticket home. Her eyes shot nervously to Renard's face.

"You'll pay me now, no absurd fees or deductions, and I'll talk and nothing more. Got it?"

Georgie shrugged helplessly at Renard. She couldn't afford to turn down that kind of money.

Joe sighed. "Fine. 3,000 American dollars is better than nothing."

"He's American?"

"He gave me American dollars and speaks with an American accent. You do the math."

Georgie stuck her hand out and Joe paid her in cold hard cash. She stuffed the money into her brassiere and ordered the men out of her dressing room. What kind of man would pay 6,000 dollars to talk to a woman?

The café was smoggy and rank with the smell of liquor. It was rare to see Georgie out and about circling the tables. Some customers recognized her face and waved as she walked by. One man gave her a flower and another grabbed her hand and whispered sexy nothings to her in French until a topless waitress appeared to serve him a drink. Georgie grabbed a glass of champagne from the woman's tray.

She sipped the drink as she walked to the VIP rooms which were a series of flimsy shade-like dividers that separated the area in cubicles away from the rest of the cafe. With the lights on, diners could watch their silhouettes from the other side.

Georgie tapped on the door then slid it open.

A tall handsome man in dark tailored pants, jacket and a black button down shirt stood on the other side of the door. The first thing she noticed was the scent of his cologne. He wore enough to fill the whole room but not so much that it was offensive. She felt a tremor of heat as his eyes followed the lines of her lips to the small of her hips. He had serious hazel-green eyes and a confident swagger as he walked toward her with the look of a man who was used to making women weak in the knees.

She threw her head back and drank the rest of her champagne in one gulp.

The man gave her an easy smile then sat on the little sofa by one of the dividers. The lights were dim, which afforded them some privacy. They were silent for a few uneasy minutes until Georgie decided to speak.

"So…did you enjoy the show?"

She was nervous and rocking on one of her heels with the empty glass in her hand.

"Absolutely. You're a talented lady."

Georgie blushed like a school girl. "Thank you…so you're American. What brings you to Paris?"

"Business," he answered vaguely.

He stared. His eyes roamed from her legs up to her soft caramel face. She was instantly uneasy. He was undressing her with his eyes.

"And you landed here?"

"Just looking for a good time."

Georgie sat her glass on the table. "I don't know what Joe told you, but you won't find it with me. Have a good night."

She turned and tried to storm out of the VIP room. But he was on her heels, blocking her from opening the sliding door. He gripped it closed with one of his hands.

"What are you doing?"

She gave him an icy stare. "Security can see everything that goes on in here."

He grazed the back of her arm with his fingertips.

"Everything?"

"Yes. And if you don't let me go, I'll call them over and have you thrown out and banned for eternity."

"Wait-I'm sorry, I didn't mean it like that."

Georgie gave him an irritated look.

"Let's cut the bullshit. What do you want

from
me?"

He took her arm and led it away from the door.

"I just want to talk. Is that okay?"

He gestured toward the little sofa and Georgie sat down. He sat beside her.

"My name is Jake. Jake Lyggle."

He waited like he expected his name to ring a bell.

"And I'm Georgine Louvelle," she shrugged.

He continued to wait, keeping her in suspense until he finally said, "Pleasure to meet you."

Jake rubbed his chin then looked up to meet her eyes again. He was nervous.

"How long have you been working here?"

"Two months."

He pressed his back against the sofa cushion and stared ahead. "And you're headlining a Burlesque? Interesting job…."

'What is this, the Spanish Inquisition?' He was beginning to get on her nerves but she answered him anyway.

"My agent called about a gig. I flew to Paris, and here I am."

"Where are you from?"

"Cornwall, Connecticut."

"Really?"

"You?"

Greenwich."

"You're kidding me! Of all the places in the world, we're from the same state?"

She gave him look like he was full of shit.

"Well, I have a house in Connecticut. But I live all over the world."

"What about Paris? You *'live here'* often?"

"Not as often as I like. And definitely not as often as I should. When can I see you again?" he asked.

"I'm not sure. I'm leaving Paris this week... thanks to you."

Jake gave her a confused look.

"The money you paid Joe. I'm using it to buy a ticket back home. I'll give him time to find a replacement and then I'm out of here. You saved my life."

He looked perturbed.

"I'm sorry, are you upset?"

"No, just surprised. To be honest, I was

hoping to spend time with you."

"You don't even know me."

He pulled her hand to his lips and kissed it.

"I know what I want when I see it. And I want you."

Georgie pulled her hand away and stood.

"I'm sorry, Mr. Lyggle, but I'm not for sale."

She walked to the door and ventured a look over her shoulder before she opened it. Jake was standing behind her, his breath warming her neck.

She spun around, ready to tell him to buzz off when he suddenly leaned forward and kissed her right on the lips. Were it someone else she would have been pissed enough to kick him in the balls or maybe use it as an opportunity to experiment with the Judo she learned in a self defense class. But this was different. This *man* was different. There was a sense of familiarity between them that she didn't quite understand. The kiss they shared was hungry and passionate, like a kiss between lost lovers finding each other after a span of a thousand years.

An ache somewhere in her soul made her want to stop. But something deeper made her want the kiss to go on forever. She was drawn to him but didn't know why. It was unnerving. Her arm shot out and pushed against his chest, putting some distance between them.

"Can I see you again?" he asked.

"I can't."

What on earth was she doing, kissing a stranger like that? She thought about Renard and wondered if he saw their silhouettes through the shade.

She met Jake's eyes, the taste of his lips still on her tongue.

"I have a boyfriend."

"That's not my problem."

Georgie opened the sliding door and escaped to the café, grateful for the rank stale air of beer and cigarettes.

She went upstairs to her apartment, showered and went to bed. But she couldn't sleep. Georgie tossed and turned the first few hours, then finally acquiesced to the fact that sleep was impossible... she stared at the ceiling until morning, thinking about Jake Lyggle, the conversation they had, and his smoldering intensity. There was something dark and mysterious about him...something mysterious *and* exciting. There was turbulence beneath his silky calm that left her longing to scratch away the surface and flirt with danger.

Nice guys were attractive, but it was the bad boys she lusted after.

Georgie finally closed her eyes at dawn's first light and fell into a sleep so heavy that it extended hours into the afternoon. She was due at the café by then, but knew she was too tired to make it.

So she called Joe and told him she was too sick to work. Surprisingly he wasn't angry and told her "Well, if you're sick, you're sick..." she could almost see him shrugging his hairy shoulders.

Renard was also warned away. She ignored his knock on the door that morning but called him later that afternoon to apologize and tell him not to stop by. His early morning visits had become a ritual. He would bring her scones and coffee, and they would cuddle on the sofa as they talked and ate. Sometimes they went for a bike ride. And true to his word even parts of the Red Light District was beautiful... not to mention historic in a way her country could never be.

Georgie was deep into her rest again when a knock on the door startled her awake. It was an urgent knock, like the person on the other side had been knocking on the door for a long time.

Georgie threw the covers back, slipped into her robe and tied it at the waist as she marched to the door. She pulled it open without looking through the peep hole. Renard was the only person who visited her anyway.

She almost fainted when she saw who was on the other side.

Georgie stared, dumbfounded as the culprit behind her sleepless night strolled into her living room.

"How---?"

"Joe gave me your apartment number," Jake said.

Georgie put her hands on her hips. Jake sat the brown paper bag he carried on her table.

She did a double take. Had he talked to Renard too? What was he doing with coffee and a bag of goods?

Jake wore a sage button down shirt and a pair of slacks. The shirt was rolled at the sleeves, showing fit arms. He looked like he had been working.

Georgie opened the paper bag and looked inside. "Apple Fritters?"

Was she going insane? She loved Apple Fritters. Would he have known that already?

"I haven't had an Apple Fritter in years."

Jake looked around. "Nice place."

"Yes it is. What are you doing here?"

"I heard you was sick and decided to stop by."

Georgie's hair was a mess about her head. She looked wild and her cheeks were hot.

Jake touched the side of her face. "But you don't look so bad."

"Well thank you for the unsolicited opinion. Can a girl take a day off without the whole world knowing about it?"

"I'm sorry-I wasn't trying to intrude."

She gave him a dubious look. "Yeah right."

"Okay—I admit it. I was trying to intrude. But I wanted to see you."

Georgie put a hand on her hip and blew an errant strand of hair from her face. "About what?"

"I'm going to Italy in a few weeks and I want you to go with me."

Her eyes popped.

"Man! Are you crazy? I just met you."

Jake smirked.

"What's with you guys and crazy propositions? I have a life, you know…I can't just pack up and dump everything to go running off with a complete stranger."

She was on a tear, but not because she was mad at him. She was mad at herself for wanting to pack up, damn it all, and follow that handsome hunk of man around the world. But why take a chance like that with a complete stranger? He could leave her stranded and she'd really be in trouble then. And of course, there was the bad boy thing…and the fact that he was frivolous enough to voraciously pursue a woman he just met. How long till he chucked her aside for someone prettier? She would be just another notch on his belt and Georgie wasn't having it.

"What's wrong? Scared to take a chance? Huh, ya big chicken?"

"I took a chance and flew to Paris and look where it got me! Besides, I can't go with you. I have a boyfriend."

She wasn't about to play arm candy to some rich dude anyway!

"You mean the French guy?"

Jake trolled around her.

"What's his name again? Roberto? Francois? Jean? Laurent? Am I warm yet?"

"You know full well what his name is."

"Is it... Renard? A beautiful woman like you can do so much better."

"Oh, you mean someone like you?"

Georgie marched to the door and opened it. "Please leave."

"You don't want me to leave and you know it. You like me." He flashed her a megawatt smile.

"I'm trying to be civil but you're making it extremely difficult."

"You call kicking me out of your apartment civil? Whew, I'd hate to see you angry."

He reached around her and slammed the door closed.

"You must think because I work at the Pink Poodle that I'm involved in the shenanigans that go on in the VIP rooms... that you can just waltz in, pay my boss for a few minutes of my time, whisk me away, have your fun then dump me?"

"Do I look like the kind of guy who would do that to you?"

"Like a typical playboy? Damned right you do."

"You told me to cut the bullshit, so I did. And now you're mad at me? Like you said, let's skip the bullshit and get to what we really want."

"And what exactly do I want Mr. Know-it all?"

She stared at him—amazed as he strolled around her apartment, lifting things, smelling her flowers, and looking at the pictures taped to the mirror on her vanity.

"My friends are flying to Paris. They'll be here tomorrow. I want you to meet them."

"I wish I never met you—much less get involved with meeting any of your friends."

"The more you resist the more obvious it is that you're attracted to me. That's all the encouragement I need."

Georgie put her hands on her hips. "Take your Fritters and get out."

Jake opened the door. "Keep them. They're your favorite, right?"

Before she could grab the fritters and throw them at his head, Jake was gone. He was making it clear that he knew more about her than she thought. She didn't know if she should be flattered or creeped out.

Georgie was left to the vapors of Jake's cologne, standing next to the door. What had come over her? She had a nice boyfriend who loved her. She was going to meet his family in Brittiny soon and if Renard was any indication they were probably wonderful people. But whether she wanted to admit it or not, something was going to happen between her and Jake... and someone was going to get their heart broken....

She didn't hear from Jake again the next morning to her relief. The last thing she needed was a confrontation between herself, Jake, and her boyfriend.

Instead, Renard came over, bringing scones, coffee, and a book. She appreciated the time he spent at her apartment and that her days weren't so lonely all the way in Paris. She hated being alone more than anything in the world.

Renard chewed the filter of his cigarette. Georgie knew he wanted to smoke but she didn't allow him to smoke cigarettes in her apartment -- especially around her clothes. She felt bad. He had nicotine shakes. Georgie covered Renard's hand with her own to stop the trembling. He put the cigarette back in the box.

"What's with you? Why so quiet today?" he asked, pushing her back against the sofa.

Georgie's eyes lit up. She smiled as his five o'clock shadow grazed the side of her face.

"I'm not quiet. Just… thinking."

"Thinking about him?"

She gave Renard a surprised look.

"Thinking about who?"

"Your friend from the VIP room. I saw you. I saw him kiss you. Did you like it?"

Georgie reached for the pack of cigarettes, which were on the table.

She put a ciggie in Renard's mouth and lit it. His body, slight as it was, was heavy on top of hers. Her bare foot dangled over the side of the sofa.

"Is this my reward?"

She gave him an annoyed look. "A reward for what?"

Renard laughed. "I don't care about the kiss. *Is only business…*"

"I didn't kiss him. He kissed me. And it had nothing to do with business."

"Then I *am* angry. What is he kissing you for?"

Georgie sighed. "He wasn't kissing me."

"What do you Americans call it then?"

"He kissed *me* and I rejected him. I told him I have a boyfriend… I told him I *love* my boyfriend."

She smiled sweetly and drew him closer.

"That sounds like a good idea. I don't like this guy."

Georgie gave Renard a surprised look. "I

didn't realize you knew each other. Why?"

"He's always hanging around, watching when you are on stage."

"Maybe he likes the show."

"I don't like the way he looks at you."

"It's not against the law to look at somebody."

Renard inhaled and blew smoke from the corner of his mouth.

"I saw him talking to Joe."

"What's wrong with that?"
"They're planning something. I think they're up to no good."

"You make it sound like a conspiracy."

Georgie took Renard's cigarette away and dropped it in a glass of water.

"When you kiss me I want to taste your lips… not your damned tobacco."

She rubbed her face against his.

"Then kiss me," Renard said.

Georgie closed her eyes and kissed him…but her thoughts were of someone else.

****

With Renard gone for the day, Georgie had time to think about Jake. She wasn't sure if she was dreading his arrival or anticipating it. Whenever there was a noise outside of her apartment, she paused, expecting him to knock on her door.

But Jake never showed up. So she took a bath, soaking in fragrant water with the book Renard had given her. Georgie turned each page, wetting them with her fingers.

When she was done she left the bath, got dressed, and went to the café thirty minutes later.

She took the stage not long after, microphone in hand and a single stream of light beaming down upon her head from the ceiling.

There was something weighing on her heart but she couldn't quite place it... She had always been that way. She would get a feeling about something... an intuition... and then something strange would happen...

Georgie scanned the audience for Jake's face but couldn't see past the stage light glaring into her eyes.

She wore a soft red gown with little beads that decorated the material with vertical glittery stripes. The dress was lengthy, backless and swung low at the shoulders in the front. She wore one side of her hair tucked behind her ear with a red orchid above it.

Singing was something she had always been able to do, even as a little girl. The one thing she would always be grateful for were parents who nurtured her artistic side as a child… until they decided she'd had enough at the tender age of six years-old. She remembered being sad about it. Sad about something she didn't quite remember. But they made it up to her when they bought her a little cat named misty.

It wasn't until a few years after high school that Georgie went to a renowned dance and acting school in New York to refine her vocal and dancing abilities.

Georgie finished her song, her gut in knots. Jake was in the audience near the center of the room. She saw him when the lights dimmed and lowered her eyes as the curtains closed.

She was standing in the same spot when Renard ran onto the stage and gave her a hug.

"That was beautiful, Georgie."

He tried to make her look up but Georgie stared at the floor. She had a feeling... something wasn't right.

"What's wrong?"

Georgie shrugged. She couldn't meet his eyes, but couldn't explain why. "I'm fine."

"Joe's asking for you. When he's done I will go to your apartment and spend the night, if that's alright with you?"

Georgie looked up this time.

"I'll bring the wine," he continued.

Renard leaned forward and Georgie gave him a kiss on the lips. It was a kiss without passion or heat, which worried her even more. One of his hands gripped her arm, the other lingered near the side of her breast.

Renard gently caressed her face. The look in his eyes when he walked away had all the fire they needed to make their relationship work. The thought consoled and troubled her at the same time.

Georgie braced herself, took a deep breath,

and left the stage. She waited for Joe to tell her off about changing the routine and not giving the audience "va-va-voom!"

But to her surprise he went on and on about her song "We are sold out. Everyone wants to see you, Georgie!"

He pulled her by the hand and led her away from the stage where the tables were situated.

"Thank you, Joe... I've been meaning to talk to you about that. With all the money you're bringing in, don't you think it's time I got a raise?"

The look on his face changed. "We not talk about money right now. We talk about it tomorrow when I go over my books. By the way, the American has asked to see you again. Go and visit his table."

At least it wasn't a trip to the VIP room again.

Georgie walked across the café to Jake's table. He sat with three guys. He stood, pulled her by the arm then leaned forward to give her a kiss. The gesture took Georgie by surprise. She looked around to see if Renard was watching but couldn't find him.

"Guys, this is Georgine, the one I've been telling you about."

He said it with a wink in his eyes. The men stood. One extended a hand.

"I'm Chris, nice to meet ya, Georgine."

"Call me Georgie, everyone else does." She smiled and Chris shot a look at Jake and smiled agreeably.

He sat down then another extended a hand. "I'm Roberto. Our other friend, Steve Hill is in Paris but he couldn't be here."

"Steve Hill? I've heard that name before. Isn't he the Connecticut State Attorney?"

"If the news rags caught wind of him in a place like this his career would be over. No offense, Georgie."

"None taken," she smiled.

Roberto sat down, clearly impressed with her easy going attitude. He shot Jake a look, nodding approval.

The third guy extended a hand. Georgie looked at his face and withdrew hers before he could take it.

Surprised, he looked at Jake, who also noticed her violent reaction to Paul.

"I know you," Georgie said. "You went to

All Savior's. You're Paul Cutter."

"Wow. I'm impressed you'd even remember me after all these years." He looked at Jake again, a questioning glance.

Georgie wasn't surprised. He looked exactly the same, only older.

"How could I forget?" Georgie folded both arms across her chest and her shoulders stiffened.

"Have a seat," Jake suggested.

He pulled Georgie's chair. She sat between Jake and Roberto.

"How's your friend? What did they call him? --Jughead? I hope he's locked away somewhere in prison, preferably, where he can't do any damage."

Paul cut a look at Jake and laughed.

"Lady you hold one mean grudge...." Paul said, slurping the shot in his glass. "How long has it been? Fifteen years?"

"What's the story with Jughead and Paul?" Chris asked.

"I went to All Savior's middle school and high school."

"We all did," Chris replied.

Georgie gave him a look of surprise.

"What a small world this is. It's like a high school reunion. Granted, I didn't know you when I was there. Were you at All Savior's?" she asked, looking at Jake.

"No."

"I still don't get it. What?" Chris repeated.

"Jughead was this kid who went to All Savior's. He made my life a living hell. Paul here, was his friend. He didn't make things any easier either. Let's just say, I will always hate Jughead and I hope I never see him again."

"That's really, *really*, interesting Jake..." Roberto replied. "I wish you had told us that, before you dragged all of us out here to Paris."

Jake shot him a hot look. "Wise ass...I don't know this Jughead kid, and from the sound of it, I never want to."

"I won't bore you guys with unresolved childhood issues. You're here to have a good time, right? I'll have the waitress bring round of drinks?"

"We're covered, sweetheart. Thanks for the offer."

Jake caressed the hair at the nape of

Georgie's neck, brushing it away from her back. A jolt of electricity shot through her body into her nethers. He absently rubbed her arm while the guys entertained her with details about their lives. But Jake, by far, was the most interesting of the gang.

Jake Lyggle was from a blue blood Connecticut family with ties to building America and some of its biggest cities dating back to the late 1700s. From railroads, to hotels, and even skyscrapers in the early 1900s, Jake's great grandfather was an architect who designed buildings from New York to Chicago.

Georgie felt ordinary by comparison. She explained how she was a child actress on a popular TV show for four years until she was replaced by another actress under circumstances she could never coax her parents to explain.

Unlike the other guys, Jake was not only unsurprised by her early TV stardom but dismissive and unimpressed. He made a face, shrugging his broad shoulders.

"I became a dance teacher but got an agent earlier this year. I was offered a role in a popular Parisian stage play in what turned out to be a burlesque show. I've been here at the Pink Poodle since… all of two and a half months."

She wondered if they were thinking the same thing she was thinking: How does one go from being the star of a TV show to headlining a sleazy burlesque in France?

She drank another round with the guys. But it was getting late and Renard was waiting for her. Georgie stood. "Well, it was nice chatting with you guys. Jake, thanks for introducing me to this crew of cool cats. I guess if the stars align, I'll meet your friend Steve another time."

She turned to walk away but Jake jumped out of his seat and grabbed her by the wrist.

"Don't leave."

"I'm tired. I'm going home."

"Can I go with you?"

She shook her head. "I'm expecting a guest."

"Is that an invitation?"

Georgie sighed. "Goodnight, Jake."

She turned and waved at the guys. They raised their glasses and bade her adieu.

That settled, Georgie looked around for Renard. She checked backstage, near the bar, the tables… she even scoured the VIP rooms. There she saw the silhouette of two men. One of the guys was short and wore a wig. She knew it was Joe. Georgie walked around and slid the door open. She wanted to ask Joe if he had seen Renard. But to her surprise Jake was inside with the older man. He gave Joe an envelope filled with cash. Suspecting they were involved in something illegal, Georgie slipped away. She went upstairs to her apartment where she washed her face and body then changed into a sexy black nightgown and waited for Renard, wondering, what Joe and Jake were involved in….

She was swishing mouthwash around in her mouth and turning the water off when she heard a loud knock on the door.

Georgie wondered if Renard remembered to bring wine glasses. The only glasses she owned were paper cups and coffee mugs.

She spat the liquid out of her mouth, wiped her face with a towel, and went to the living room to open the door. Jake was on the other side.

His eyes moved from her feet to the top of her head slowly. She waited for him to speak – and for all of thirty seconds, he seemed at a loss for words.

"What on earth are you doing here? You have to go—*now*. I told you I was expecting someone."

She was about to close the door in his face when Jake brushed her aside and walked in. "What happened with you and Paul Cutter?"

"I already told you. Now will you get out?" Georgie pointed toward the door.

Jake fixed her with a stare. "What did his friend do to make you so upset? There's more to this story and I want to hear it."

He seemed genuinely perplexed and angry.

"It's a long story and I don't feel like getting emotional right now. Will you leave? I'm serious."

"Damn your boyfriend for a minute," he said, seating himself on the sofa. "Tell me what happened and I'll leave. I'm not trying to hurt you but I have to know."

Georgie sighed. "I'll tell you but you have to go—immediately after, okay?"

Jake agreed.

"When I was twelve, my parents used residuals from my acting jobs to pay for my education. They sent me to All Saviors Private School. We lived walking distance, unlike some of the other kids who happened to live on campus in the boarding rooms."

"I know all about All Saviors. Get to the part where Paul and his friend supposedly did something to hurt you."

"Supposedly?"

"The part where he offended you, Georgie."

"I met a lot of kids, many who knew me from the show. I was a popular happy child, except when Jughead was around. Needless to say, he lived up to his name. He threw rocks at me, chased me home from school, threw my books into puddles, and had even chased me with two of his Rottweiler dogs."

"Sounds like a typical bully. I know it probably hurt but you seem like you're having trouble moving beyond what Jughead did. We've all met bullies at some point in our lives. I know I did."

Georgie sighed. "I have every right to hate him after all these years."

"What did he do to you, Georgie?"

"—He killed my cat. What kind of psychopath would kill a little girl's cat?

"Her name was Misty. My parents gave her to me when I was six. I know you might be thinking, well… it's just a pet. But Misty was a part of our family."

Jake waited for Georgie to continue. She took a deep breath, collecting herself.

"Then Jughead killed her."

"How do you know he killed her? Maybe she chased a squirrel into the street."

"Why would make you say that? Misty didn't chase squirrels! Jake, my parents had to remind me over and over again that she was gone. I'd wake up, expecting Misty to jump on the foot of my bed. I'd call out, look for her around the house and our backyard until… they'd remind me that Misty wasn't here. I cried for weeks. I knew he had something to do with it. My father said some kid chased her into street. That she'd been hit by a car. My father gave a perfect description of Jughead. I called animal services and the police to report it, but because I didn't remember seeing her get hit the police never pursued animal cruelty charges. I'll never forgive him – ever. Luckily he never spoke to me or bothered me again after that. He transferred to a new school and I never saw him again. It upsets me to think about him."

"Why?"

She shrugged, biting back tears. "I don't know…."

Georgie wiped her eyes and sniffled. "I feel so ridiculous, crying about a stupid cat!"

She buried her face in her hands, unable to look at Jake.

"I'm just glad it wasn't something worse — are you sure you never saw him again? Maybe you're not crying about the cat. Maybe you're upset about something else?"

She looked up at Jake. "I'm positive. Why are you asking me that?"

Jake scooted close to Georgie and wrapped an arm around her shoulders. "I'm sorry about your cat. And I'm sorry Jughead gave you a hard time. I'm really, really sorry."

"It's over now. I feel so stupid," she sobbed.

"Don't cry," he coaxed, draping an arm around her shoulders.

His lips brushed against the side of her face then slid to the curve of her neck. She closed her eyes, falling into his seductive trap until she remembered Renard and the wine he was supposed to bring over. This was supposed to be *their* night. Jake could charm the skin off a snake. What in the hell was she thinking, letting this man seduce her like that?

Flustered, Georgie pressed a hand against his chest. "STOP!"

"What's wrong?"

She adjusted her gown. "I told you what you wanted to know. Now you need to honor your end of the agreement and leave...NOW."

"Why?"

"I'm expecting someone."

"Don't worry about him."

"Dammit, Jake. I have a boyfriend!"

"I thought I was your boyfriend," he

smiled.

Georgie couldn't help but laugh.

"Don't be ridiculous. I'm serious."

He gave her a steady look.

"You want me as much as I want you. You don't have to hide it."

She gave him an angry look.

"I'm not hiding anything! I don't want you, Jake. You're delusional—out of your damned mind… I'm serious—I told you my boyfriend is coming over. Now what if he were to walk in and catch us?"

"Catch us doing what? Having an affair?"

Jake kissed her again, this time softly on the shoulder. She closed her eyes as his fingers caressed her spine.

"We're not having an affair," she moaned.

"Then what are we doing?"

Jake pulled Georgie from the sofa and carried her to bed. She wanted to kick herself for being so damned weak. Jake was right. She wanted him. She wanted him badly. Twice, she'd forgotten all about Renard, much as she loved him. *Did she love him?* What was it about her that made her want to destroy the beautiful friendship and romance she was building with Renard? Was it her way of leaving him behind? She was moving back to the States. A relationship between her and Renard would never work, right? Or was that just a convenient excuse?

"Renard will be here any minute now," she said aloud, though reminding herself.

"No he won't."

Georgie laid her head against her pillow and closed her eyes. Jake laid beside her and took his jacket off.

"Just say 'no' and I'll leave."

Georgie opened an eye and stole a peek at his face. "Liar."

"I'm not the liar, G. I can see it in your eyes. You want me to stay."

"What? You're crazy."

She rolled her eyes.

"I've got you all figured out…"

He ran a hand over the swell of her breasts then kissed her lips.

"When you look at me sometimes you get this focused expression on your pretty face… then you turn away when I catch you looking."

"And what are my eyes saying to you now?"

"They're saying, 'make love to me, Jake'."

He said it in a fake falsetto voice. Georgie smiled.

"Then what are you waiting for?" she whispered.

****

Making love to Jake was everything Georgie imagined it would be. She lay beside him; the aftershock of hot passionate sex ricocheting through her body. She couldn't help but wonder what in the hell had come over her... she was on the edge now, everything was all screwed up.

Jake closed his eyes and traced circles on her shoulders with his finger. Words couldn't describe how she felt at that moment. She felt euphoric yet sad. She knew she would have to end things with Renard if he found out. She also knew things would end between her and Jake when it was time for her to go back to the States. It was a lose-lose situation. She had no idea where her

Renard was, he was a few hours late. She supposed, he wasn't coming at all. Which wasn't a bad thing.

"You still didn't answer my question."

She looked at Jake, trying to remember what he asked her. "What?"

"About going with me to Italy."

Georgie sighed. "I can't, I told you already."

"Why not?"

"I've never been to Italy."

"So."

She thought about seeing Jake and Joe in the VIP room.

"I – don't trust you," she mumbled.

"So you're in the habit of sleeping with men you don't trust?"

Georgie reached across the bed and slapped Jake hard across the cheek with her pillow.

He sat up, ear ringing.

"What in the hell did you do that for?"

"Don't ever talk to me like again. I told you before, I'm not one of Joe's so called 'courtesans'... as a matter of fact—just get out."

Georgie tried to climb out of bed but Jake's arms were around her waist, pulling her back.

"I'm sorry...G, damn. I was just kidding around. I won't do it again."

"Yeah right."

"I'll prove it.

"How?"

"Let me take you to Italy."

"I said no. I'm not running off to Italy with you or anybody else. What if you leave me stranded and alone in a foreign country?"

"Is that what you're worried about?"

"Wouldn't you worry about the same thing if you were in my shoes?"

"I would never, ever, leave you stranded, G, and I would never leave you. Whatever is happening between us will last as long as we want it to last. There's no expiration date on what I feel for you right now.

"What you *do* feel? Lust?"

He touched her face. "I feel like you are a beautiful, *amazing* woman. Why can't you see that? I wouldn't be here if I didn't care about you."

Georgie blushed like a school girl on crack.

Her smile was ear to ear. She leaned over to kiss him when suddenly there was a knock on the door. Georgie froze.

"I'll answer it…"

Jake moved to get out of bed but Georgie grabbed his arm and slapped a hand over his mouth. She was sure it was Renard. He probably had a late night at the café. She looked at the clock, it was 2 a.m.

Had he gotten to her earlier it would have been Renard in her bed and not Jake. Strange how things turned out, she thought. How difficult it was to be torn between two men…much less, admit who already had her body, heart, *and* soul.

Renard knocked again and this time it was more insistent.

Jake moved her hand aside. "Tell him or I will."

"Please don't!"

"You have enough money to go home. Tell Joe you resign and go with me to Italy."

"I told you I can't go away with you!"

"I'm doing you a favor. Somebody has to tell this fool so we might as well do it now."

Jake moved to get out of bed but Georgie

grabbed his arm and gave him a pleading look.

"I'll go to Italy with you! Just be quiet!"

She couldn't bear hurting Renard this way. He didn't deserve it. She could slip away without ever seeing his face again.

"Je sais que vous êtes dedans là. Sortez et combattez comme un home!"

She listened as his muffled voice filtered through the door.

"Ouvrez la porte ou je la forcerai pour s'ouvrir!"

Georgie slapped a hand over her mouth.

"What did he say?" Jake asked.

"He said, *'I know you're in there. Come out and fight like a man.'*"

"What else?"

"*Open the door or I'll kick it in.'*"

"I swear on my mother's grave, if he kicks that door in... I'm going medieval on the fucker. Got it?"

"I-I got it, just... calm down."

"Tell him to beat it or *I will*."

"Please, enough Jake! He's hurting... I can't believe I did this to him. I can't believe

I would do this to anyone...*Why*?" It was like Jake had her mesmerized. She was appalled by her own behavior, but couldn't stop.

Georgie shook her head and covered her face with both of her hands. The situation was bad enough without Jake ranting like a mad lunatic.

Jake settled back, calming down. "I don't like this. We're leaving tomorrow."

Georgie fished around her pillow for one of Renard's cigarette, found a lighter then lit it.

She said nothing in response to Jake's demand but realized it was time to go. She couldn't face Renard again, not after how badly she humiliated and cheated on him. She had the money she needed to get home anyway. She could slither out of the building first thing in the morning.

Italy wasn't an option.

Jake took the cigarette out of her hand and stubbed it on Joe's wooden table.

"And no more of these." He stared her straight in the eye. "I can't blame him for being hurt. I know firsthand how devastated a man would be to lose you."

CHAPTER FIVE

At the first sign of dawn Georgie was out of bed. She left Jake to his sleep and took a shower. When she was done, she gathered her belongings and packed them into her suitcases. She was tired but the bulk of her work was done. She climbed back in bed and slept another hour. She could hardly keep her eyes open. Jake's arm rested heavily around her waist. The alarm was blaring when she woke up again.

"Did you set the clock?"

"I did, sorry about that." He climbed out of bed then stepped into his pants. As he walked across the room toward the bathroom, he noticed her suitcases near the door.

"So you're going to Italy with me?"

He smiled and Georgie was dead all over again. She wanted to rush him and tell him 'yes', but had the sense to know that a relationship between them would never work.

"I'm going home. I already showered and packed my suitcases. I'm leaving in an hour and hopping the first plane back to the States. I just want to thank you. Without your help, I wouldn't have enough money to get home."

She could tell he was disappointed by the expression on his face.

"You call this thanking me?"

He went into the bathroom. Georgie could hear him peeing then washing his hands. She wrinkled her nose then stepped into her clothes. He turned the shower on. She was tempted to quietly slip away to avoid another confrontation with Jake about going with him to Italy, until she heard the shower turn off a few minutes later. She was fully dressed when he came out, towel around his waist.

He used his cell phone to arrange a ride to the airport then dressed himself in last night's clothes. Georgie walked to the door and Jake grabbed her suitcases, leaving her with a shoulder bag.

Georgie waited until he was out of the

apartment then locked the door behind them. She left the key in the lock. It wasn't' the smartest thing to do but at least Joe would get his key back.

The walk down the stairs of the building was somber. She felt like a scarlet woman…. They were at the foot of the stairway when Georgie noticed a long black car in front of the building. A driver in a black uniform and matching hat stood before the back passenger door, waiting.

"Is that our ride?"

"Yeah, I'll have him put your bags in the trunk."

Georgie opened the door and walked out. She strode ahead to Jake's car hoping she wouldn't run into Joe. The last thing she wanted to do on top of everything else was explain why she was abandoning the show. Not that she should care when he wasn't paying her fairly anyway.

She had made it halfway to the car, Jake beside her, when someone approached them from behind. She turned and saw Renard coming around from the alley.

He had a brown paper bag and two cups

of coffee in his hands. His hair was dirty like he had yet to take a shower, his eyes were bloodshot, and he had a five o' clock shadow on his face. Like Jake, he was wearing last night's clothes. The look he gave Georgie broke her heart to pieces.

"*Georgine...*" he called.

Jake nudged her in the back. "Keep walking."

The driver gave them a curious grin and took Georgie's bag before opening the door. She tried not to look at Renard and stepped one of her heeled shoes into the car.

The seats were leathery and soft. The driver's side of the car was on the right side, unlike American cars, which were on the left.

"Georgine!" Renard called again.

She looked up, unable to look away any longer.

"I bought coffee."

He gestured helplessly with the coffee and bag of scones as she sat down and the driver closed the door. Jake shrugged and was on his way around to the other side of the car as the driver walked to the back and put Georgie's luggage in the trunk.

Renard tapped on her window.

"You think you can hurt someone and just walk away?"

Jake, who was about to sit down saw Renard looking into the window. He climbed out and looked over the hood... "Get away from the car," Jake warned.

Renard shot him a dirty look and backed away.

"You filthy harlot..."

Georgie rolled the window down. Why couldn't he let it go? Why not make it easier on them both and move on with his life?

"I didn't mean to hurt you."

"But you did. You think I didn't see what you were up to? You think I didn't know he paid Joe to make me work late so he could steal *my* girl? We were supposed to go to Brittany. What about our plans? Huh?"

"I'm sorry... I didn't mean-"

"You didn't mean it? I have never heard anything so stupid in my life. Did he accidentally fall into your bed?"

"I'm sorry..."

Having enough of Renard, Jake walked around the car.

"Look, I told you to back off. Leave her alone. She made her choice. You're just pissed because it wasn't you."

Jake pushed Renard hard in the chest.

He stumbled over a crack in the sidewalk and fell to the ground, spilling the two cups of coffee onto his shirt.

"Jake, please get in the car," Georgie said.

Jake walked back to the car, opened her door and told her to slide over. Renard watched as the dark tinted window rolled up.

Georgie turned and glared at Jake as the car sped through the streets of Paris toward the airport.

"Is it true? Did you pay Joe to make him work late?"

"You honestly think I had something to do with that man's work schedule? It's sour grapes, G. He's blaming everyone else because he was dumb enough to let you get away. I should feel sorry for him I guess, but it's not my problem. I want to be with you. The best man won."

"Won? What is this, a competition?"

She turned and looked out the window,

seeing parts of Paris she didn't remember seeing in route to The Pink Poodle.

"Can we drive around the Eiffel Tower before I go to the airport? I want to see Paris before I go."

She remembered at one time wanting to see Paris with Renard. Nevertheless, the worst part was over. As humiliating a confrontation that it was, she didn't have to lie or hide what she felt anymore. She leaned toward Jake and laid her head on his shoulder. He was surprised, judging by the expression on his face. Perhaps a bit relieved.

"We can do anything you want. In fact, I'll show you everything you deserve to see in Paris."

Jake ordered the driver to take them to the Ritz Hotel, where he and his friends all had rooms on the same floor. She tried not to react when they got out of the car and walked into the posh hotel. She felt inappropriate. It was too much of an extreme, going from Pigalle Street to the upscale hotel.

Jake took her to the Coco Chanel suite. He

sat her luggage near the door and told her to make herself at home.

Georgie walked to the window and looked down. The view was breathtaking.

He stood behind her and slipped his arms around her waist. She felt his breath against her hair.

"You can see the Tuileries Palace and the Louvre. At night, the lights are spectacular."

He gestured toward the courtyard, the ancient museum, and the centuries old building just beyond the Place Vendome.

Georgie knew it was a subtle invitation to stay. To be with Jake and in Paris seemed like more than she deserved.

Jake left Georgie to gaze out of his window while he showered again and changed clothes. When he returned, she had taken her shoes off and was sitting on the sofa, feet curled beneath her.

Jake sat beside her and opened his laptop.

"I hope you don't mind but I have some work to do. Get changed, we're going out as soon as I'm done."

He hammered away on the keyboard of his laptop while Georgie stood before him and took off her dress.

"Should I change in here?"

Jake looked up.

"Or should I change somewhere else?"

Georgie took the laptop out of his hands and set it aside. She sat on his lap and straddled him, sinking her feet into the cushions of the sofa. She gave him a sly smile.

It was the first time she had ever seen him blush.

"I have to get some work done. Sorry, honey."

"Fine..."

Georgie gave him a long smoldering kiss then climbed from his lap. She had to pry his hand from her backside before he grabbed his laptop and started typing again. She walked to the bedroom and paused in the doorway, flaunting her figure and derriere in the black bra and lace panties she wore.

"Let me know when you're done."

Georgie walked inside and collapsed on the king sized bed. She heard the door slam behind her. Jake had followed her in.

"So much for work..." he said.

The bed cushion sunk under his weight. They made love again, this time it was even better than the night before.

An hour later, Jake was typing on his laptop while Georgie flipped through the pages of a French magazine. He bought and sold stock, made appointments, and had telephone conferences without even putting his pants on. By late afternoon she was out of her mind with boredom until Jake was finally done.

They showered, got dressed and toured the city, first visiting the Louvre Museum. They entered through the glass Pyramid in the courtyard and took pictures of each other inside and outside of the structure.

On the tour, Georgie studied Greek sculptures, unable to contain her amazement of the detail and age of the statues. She mused to Jake how brilliant the Greeks were and wondered how they achieved the human-likeness of their pieces. Jake assured her that despite the lack of visible technology, artistically the Greeks were an advanced society and could rival today's society not only with its knowledge of sculpting, but astronomy… much like the Egyptians. They moved to Renaissance paintings and Egyptian artifacts…anything Georgie wanted to see.

When she with done with the tour they took a walk around the square and continued deep into the city. They visited shops and bought souvenirs then stopped for a rest near a fountain where they sat and kissed.

The fountain spouted water from the arms of a stone sculpture in the shape of the goddess Venus. Coins glistened at the bottom of the surrounding pond. Georgie left the bench and tip toed over dry pigeon droppings, climbed onto the fountain and dropped coins inside. They closed their eyes and made a wish while Jake held her hand to keep her from falling into the water.

"What did you wish for?" Georgie asked.

They held hands. Georgie walked on top of the thick stone railing surrounding the fountain, Jake on dry ground.

"We'll know when we get to Italy whether my wish came true."

"Is that your wish?"

"Maybe."

He kept a straight face and pulled her down.

They went to dinner afterwards, then to Jake's hotel suite at the Ritz. Georgie was exhausted, and went to bed straightaway while Jake sat at his desk and worked till midnight.

The next morning she was shaking him awake. Jake opened his eyes to breakfast. They had fruit, croissants, berries, crepes, camembert, brie and crackers with piping hot tea.

She massaged Jake's shoulders while he typed on his laptop and ate strawberry crepes.

"Do you always work on vacation?"

"I have business here and in Italy… then I'm going back to the States. So technically, it's not a vacation."

Georgie sighed. He closed his eyes, rested the back of his head against her chest then kissed her hand.

"I thought you were here on holiday?"

"I schedule vacations between trips. Now it's time to get back to work."

"So you were squeezing me in when you went to the Pink Poodle?"

He was typing again.

"No. I was squeezing business in. It had been my intention to visit our Paris office for a while."

"Did you see everything you came to see?"

He shrugged her away. "Yeah, I think so." Georgie slithered back in bed and finished her breakfast. It was time to think about going home. The last thing she wanted was for Jake to take her for granted.

Jake's eyes were fixed on the computer screen. "I called a few shops and set up a line of credit for you. They'll bill it to my credit card. The list is on the table. Have at it and go shopping."

She couldn't mute her surprise if she tried. "I have my own clothes."

"You look good, babe, but you're in the fashion capital of the world. You might as well look like it."

Georgie shrugged. "When in Rome I guess…"

"Speaking of which, we're going to Rome next week."

"When you invited me to Italy I had no idea you meant Rome. You still want me to go?"

He turned to look at her. "Of course. I want you to go with me now more than ever."

Rome was one of the many places she had always wanted to visit. But it was too much. What was this about anyway? A shopping spree and a trip across Europe? Was he looking for a traveling companion?

"I can't go shopping because I'm going home."

He sat the laptop aside.

"Why? I told you I made plans for us."

"I feel like I won a Clearinghouse sweepstakes. I don't want an all expense paid trip through Europe. Jake, I want to be sure my feelings for you are genuine. And I want to make sure your feelings for me are the same."

She held his hand.

"Did I say anything about doubting your feelings?"

"No."

"Don't leave... Let's go back to the States together."

He rubbed her thigh.

"Now?"

"After the trip to Italy. Is that okay? I don't mean to pressure you. I just need to have you with me."

She was flattered. He made her feel so important.

"Fine, I'll stay..."

"Good. I'm not working too much? I'm not neglecting you, am I?"

"Yes, but work is work. It has to be done. I'll visit a few shops like you said and leave you to do whatever it is you're doing. I know you were just trying to get rid of me so you can

 work in peace."

He kissed her then resumed typing.

True to Jake's word, a week later, they were traveling the ancient streets of Rome. Jake booked a room at a hotel which sat over the famous Spanish Steps. The view of the city from there was breathtaking. The architecture, buildings, churches, statues, and fountains, were beautiful, majestic, and ancient. Rome's culture helped shape modern democracies, Georgie thought.... She was humbled by the fact that her eyes were looking at more than two thousand years of history. There were structures still standing and some of them crumbling that were older than the whole country of America.

Jake was probably equally overwhelmed, wanting to concentrate on the beauty around them. She noticed he hadn't touched her since their arrival in Rome, short of holding her hand or kissing her on the cheek. He seemed distant.

"How long will we be in Italy?"

"A few more weeks."

"Weeks? What kind of business is keeping us here this long?" She wanted to gripe about the fact that he had done little more than kiss her on the forehead that morning, but decided against it. She was also homesick, but not quite sick enough to leave him behind. She felt scarily attached.

"I'm overseeing the construction of our new building. Technically, the project has already been completed but there are a few loose ends to tie up. And as mundane as it sounds, I'm also here to move our other Rome office from a paper filing system to computers. It was one of the endless things my parents didn't get to do before they died. I'm meeting with security analysts, of course. There's a lot of money moving around so the system will need to be secure."

Georgie imagined him managing all of the Lyggle subdivisions down to the minutest detail.

"You didn't tell me your parents died. I'm sorry…."

"It's fine. I miss them, but at least I get to live my own life and choose the person I want to be with."

He touched her face.

Georgie wondered what Jake meant. She laid a hand on his forehead and checked his temperature. He looked tired and overworked.

"Sounds like a huge undertaking. You're not burned out, are you?"

"I'm fine."

He moved her hand aside and kissed the

tips of her fingers.

"Lyggle Corp. was in terrible shape when they passed away. The company was almost bankrupt. But that was roughly five years ago. Everything is back on track now. Last year, we were up billions of dollars in profit."

"What is your title at Lyggle Corporation? What do you do?"

"I own it."

"A part of it or the whole thing?"

"All of it."

"Ooooh, impressive..." she massaged his shoulders. "But it sounds sooo boring. Do you ever have time for yourself? Maybe you should hire somebody to help you with some of this stuff? Someone to take care of things when you want to relax."

He rubbed the silky material of her gown and covered one of her breasts with his hand. Her body hungered for more.

"I have you."

"Seriously,   Jake..."
"I have assistants, people who run parts of the corporation as a whole. But I try to be as involved as possible. That's where my

parents went wrong. They were socialites. Blue bloods through and through. But they didn't know anything about business or investing…"

"But you did."

"Of course I did. I tried to convince them, but they were wrapped up in their own personal bullshit. They let people who didn't have their best interests at heart do the work for them and screwed up."

"But the company's fine now, right? You're working too hard."

"I'm almost done, Georgie. Give me another week and I promise to relax and spend more time with you."

They kissed for several minutes. Georgie put her arms and legs around Jake and drew him closer. His body was hard against her soft flesh. She moaned as they kissed hoping he would finally sate her desires until Jake tore himself away and moved her arms from around his neck.

"I'm gonna get some sleep. I have an early day tomorrow."

He rolled over and Georgie sighed.

"Guess I'll be visiting the ruins by myself... *again.*"

CHAPTER SIX

She spent the next few days touring nearby ruins and buying souvenirs with the three thousand dollars Joe had given her. Jake deigned to arrange a line of credit for her at Robeiro's...a fancy Italian shop. Georgie supposed it was to keep her busy while he was working but decided not to accept his offer. She was reduced to pinching pennies left and right but she felt like an independent woman spending her own money; self-reliance being worth its weight in gold. To rely on Jake defeated the purpose of leaving the States. She left to see the world, live on her own, and most importantly, to escape her parents. It was Georgie's point not to call Louis and Irma Louvelle after leaving France. Never mind that she was a twenty eight-year old woman with a twenty-four year old younger sister in Anne who lived on her own and worked as a junior executive at a pharmaceutical company.

Georgie's meager accomplishments were barely comparable to that of her sister's, who at worst had something she truly desired in having earned their parent's trust and confidence.

Louis and Irma just couldn't seem to loosen their grip. In their eyes Georgie was 'tenuous...' were her father's words, 'and easy to break'. She was tired of arguments that more than often reduced her to tears or coerced her into doing whatever her parents wanted. How deeply it hurt to know they saw her as weak and needing of their supervision. She sometimes despised herself because of them, often looking into a mirror and seeing the same weaknesses she'd seen reflecting in their eyes reflecting back from her own.

Louis and Irma weren't bad people but quite the opposite. They loved their daughter and wanted to trust her... but there were secrets in Georgie's past. Secrets her parents kept as if to protect her delicate mind from fracturing into empty shells.

Georgie went back to the hotel after hours of sightseeing Rome without Jake.
It was a peculiar empty feeling having spent a whole day traveling a strange country

alone and not having anyone to share her excitement with. But it also gave her time to herself. And time to think about her relationship with Jake.

It was dark when she walked into the hotel suite. Save for a twinkling of light that glowed from a distant skyline into the wall to wall landscape windows. The light made shadowy flickering motions in the room.

She sat her shopping bags down and kicked her shoes off. Her feet sank into the thick carpeting. Georgie wondered if they were going to swell after walking around in heels all day.

The subtle smell of smoke filled her nostrils. She sneezed and walked to the window and looked out, wondering if someone had lit a bonfire and the smell had floated in through the windows.

She took in the view then flinched when a hand gripped her upper arm and turned her around.

"Where were you?" Jake said.

Georgie sighed in relief.

"You startled me..." she panted.

She met his hazel-green eyes. Jake waited

for her to answer.

"Site seeing."

"All day?"

"Is there anything else to do around here?"

She didn't like his tone. Georgie shirked out of Jake's grasp and left the window.

"I thought you were going to Robeiro's?"

"I changed my mind," she snapped.

"I waited two hours for you to show up."

"And here I am, waiting twelve hours a day for you night after night. What's your point?"

He sighed. "I ordered a candlelit dinner."

There were plates and two waned candles on the dining table. She could almost make out their dinner. The sauce on their plates looked cold and stiff and the champagne was flat.

Georgie shrugged. She reached for the lamp but Jake grabbed her hand.

"Is there something you need to say?"

"I don't know. What do you want me to say to you?"

"I'm sorry would do just fine."

Georgie gave Jake an incredible look. "I have nothing to apologize for."

She tried to shake out of his grasp but Jake held firm. He yanked and pulled her toward the door. The stench of alcohol was on his breath.

He grabbed a card from the table and put it in front of her face.

She read the name. *Marcello Giordano*.

"What is this?"

"Were you with him?"

"First of all, I don't know who *he* is."

"Then what's his business card doing here?"

"How in the hell am I supposed to know? Maybe it's an advertisement left by the cleaning lady or by concierge or whoever else comes in here while we're gone."

"So now you take me for an idiot? I've been at a guest at this hotel on and off for years, Georgie and I have never seen a card like this. First 'Renard' and now you're running around on me. "

"Running around on you?"

"So I guess all that talk about refusing to let men buy you was bullshit. I guess Marcello was the highest bidder this time."

There was a cold and bitter look in his

eyes. "So are you? Are you running around on me?"

Georgie gave him a hurt look, snatched her arm away and stormed to the bedroom. She grabbed her empty suitcases, threw them on the bed and began to pack her clothes inside.

Jake walked in behind her and closed the suitcase she was stuffing.

"Don't touch me and don't touch my got'damned suitcases."

"So you're *leaving me* stranded and alone in Italy? Great *Georgie*."

She gave him an incredulous look. "Exactly. I'm leaving you for the highest bidder, remember?" Her hands were trembling and her body quaked with anger. She was seeing a side of Jake that she hadn't seen before and didn't like it.

Georgie pulled her suitcases from the bed and left the room. Jake followed, took the luggage from her hand and blocked the door.

"I wasn't insulting you and I didn't ask you to leave."

"You weren't insulting me?" she gasped.

"You promised you wouldn't do this the first night went spent together in France and I believed you."

She tried to open the door but Jake slammed it closed.

"You're not leaving until you talk to me."

They glared at each other in mini standoff. He blocked her from going out; she blocked him from keeping her in. His chest rose and fell as if out of breath.

"I don't like jealous men."

"Then don't do anything to make me jealous."

He stared her down, the hard look in his eyes softening.

"You're right... I broke my promise. I'm sorry, G'."

"Thank you. Now please get out of my way," Georgie replied.

"I apologize for everything I said tonight. It was uncalled for... I don't want you to leave."

"I guess you can't get everything you want, Jake," Georgie answered.

"I know," he solemnly replied. "You won't get a flight on short notice at this time of night. You can stay until morning if you want." He looked panicked. "I had no right to accuse you or grab you like that. I hope you understand, Georgie. *But I need to have you with me.* I can't bear the thought of losing you. When you were gone I-"

Georgie silenced him with a hand over his lips. Seeing Jake vulnerable, remorseful, and broken reminded her of how tender and sweet he could be. She had known from the beginning that he had anger issues…just not a display as serious as she'd seen tonight. But she could change him, couldn't she?

CHAPTER SEVEN

The next morning, Jake was gone when Georgie woke up. She glanced past the empty space on his side of the bed and looked at the nightstand. There was a note.

Georgie hesitated to open the folded sheet of paper. She drew the blanket to her neck, pressed her back against the headboard and took a deep breath. Her hands trembled. The mere thought of their relationship coming to an end sent tears rushing to her eyes. She remembered the lingering smell of alcohol on his breath the night before and knew he was drunk and not thinking clearly. She had already forgiven him.

Georgie opened the letter... though it was less a letter than a list of instructions.

"Pack your bags and wait at the top of the Spanish Steps at ten."

She was in agony. What did it mean? 'Curse him for being so damned mysterious!' She checked the clock. It was almost nine. With an errant beat to her heart, Georgie hurried away, showered, and got dressed.

When she was done she finished packing her bags, fretting over what was to come and lamenting her decision not to run back home in the first place.

Her heart was on the line.

Rather, it was caught in her throat when she opened Jake's closet and saw that his luggage was gone.

It was obvious from the lack of attention given her in the weeks they'd been in Italy, the fact that they hadn't made love, and their fight the night before meant he just wasn't interested anymore and was looking for an excuse to back out.

Georgie sat on the bed and tried to quiet her thoughts. She felt shrill... and silly. He wanted her to wait on the Spanish Steps for the car he was sending to take her to the airport. Yes... that was it. Just like 'that!' it was over.

A knock on the door snapped Georgie awake from the turmoil quietly building within her. It was a bus boy. He said something to her in Italian and gestured toward her luggage. She gave him the signal to take the bags away. He put her belongings on a little cart and pushed the items out of the room. Georgie grabbed her shoulder bag and followed, a tear pricking the corner of her eye as she walked out.

The bus boy was kind enough to walk her to the Spanish Steps, which were nearby, just outside of the hotel.

Georgie stood at the very top looking down. She tried to keep a straight face but felt gutted. Jake had done exactly what she was afraid he would do. Abandon her in a strange country. He didn't even have the decency to tell her face to face.

The market was busy. Pedestrians and camera-happy tourists climbed the stairs in droves. She tried not to look at a pair of lovers sitting nearby, entwined in each other's arms reading a book. The centuries-old steps were in a high traffic metropolitan part of Rome. The crowds were unbearable and the weather was hot.

Georgie sat down at the very top of the steps and pulled her skirt over her knees. Before she knew it she was sobbing her heart out, drawing curious stares from pedestrians passing her by.

"Are you okay?"

A gentleman with a thick Italian accent propped his foot atop the stair she was sitting on and offered her a handkerchief.

Georgie sobbed and took it out of his hands. She wiped at the mascara making a trail from her eyes and looked at his face. He was all of twenty-five years old-if that, but very cute, with dark hair.

"No, everything is not okay!" she cried. "Do I look okay to you?"

"I'm sorry, I didn't mean anything by it. You were crying..."

"I know what I was doing! Can a girl have a little privacy? Must you stand there and eyeball me like that?"

"Privacy in a busy place like this? Maybe you shouldn't be crying in public if you don't want people watching you."

His eyes flashed her a hot look.

Georgie sighed. "What do you want?"

"Are you Georgine Louvelle?"

She looked at the man, surprised. "Who are you?"

"You see that vehicle at the bottom of the steps? I'm going to carry your bags down there and you are going to get into the car and go with me. You may leave your hot temper outside of my vehicle, please."

He grabbed her three suitcases and climbed down the stairs two at a time before she could reply.

"What are you waiting for? Get your bag and come on. I don't have all day."

He turned and continued down.

Georgie ran after her luggage, following the man down the stairs. She had enough to worry about without some thief stealing her bags, or worse, kidnapping her and holding her for ransom.

She finally caught up at the bottom of the steps.

"First of all, I don't even know who you are. You expect me to get into some car with you?"

"Your boyfriend, Mr. Lyggle paid for my services. You either get in or I leave you here."

"What's your name?"

"Marcello Giordano from Giordano Tours and Services."

She remembered his name from the night

before and the mystery about how his card had gotten into the suite.

He opened the back door of the car and flipped her luggage inside. The car was small and black with a high cabin. It was an older model, like something from the 1950s.

"Well, Marcello… may I see some identification? Maybe a license for your car service?"

Marcello scoffed and went into the vehicle. He opened the glove compartment box and handed her the requested documentation.

Georgie skimmed the details then gave it back to Marcello. He held the door open and waited for her to go inside.

It was Jake's way of getting back at her. To not only break up with her, but hiring the man he suspected her of cheating on him with.

Soon Marcello and Georgie were skirting through the streets of Rome, past its basilicas and old world architecture… she watched and even took pictures. They were mementos to remember her time in Rome with Jake. Georgie stopped when they passed a sign directing them to the airport.

"Excuse me, where are we going? We passed the sign directing us to the airport a half mile ago."

"We are not going to the airport," he replied.

"Then where are we going?"

"To the villa where your boyfriend is waiting for you."

Georgie sat back in her seat. Her heart leapt. Jake was waiting for her at an Italian villa. She felt like a fool. She had fallen into utter despair when she saw that his suitcases were gone.

"Thanks, Marcello… I'm sorry, I think we got off to a bad start earlier. Are you going to be our tour guide? What kind of villa is it?"

"Ah, so now you are full of questions, are you?"

He had a smug look on his face. Georgie rolled her eyes.

"Just answer the question."

"It's a lakeside villa. You'll find the lake has an interesting history… as it was formed by a volcanic crater tens of thousands of years ago. The villa is a beautiful place in a beautiful region of Rome. It is not very far from the Vatican State."

"Is that where the Pope lives?"

Marcello looked over his shoulder at Georgie and gave her a bit of "side eye". She felt a little stupid for even asking.

"Yes, it's the home of the catholic church. A separate state within Italy ruled by the Pope."

"How far away is it from Rome?"

"It is in the heart of our Rome, Bella, not very big but a few blocks long."

She smiled at his use of such a casual address... *"Bella"*.

"If you wish to renew our acquaintance, I happily accept. I shouldn't be angry about your reaction at the Spanish Steps. You were distraught and I disturbed you."

Georgie was red with embarrassment. "Yes, I was. I'm sorry. I didn't mean to take it out on you."

"It's water under the bridge, Bella. If you don't mind my asking, were you crying about your boyfriend? Did you think he ran away from you?"

"How did you--?"

"You thought we were going to the

airport, that's how. No man in his right mind would dump a beautiful woman like you in a city swimming with strong Italian men," Marcello laughed.

"How far away is it?"

"About an hour and a half away. You had an eventful morning, we'll stop soon for some lunch. You like Italian food, don't you?"

"Of course! Who doesn't?" Georgie smiled. She was famished. She didn't eat dinner the night before and was too upset to eat breakfast.

They drove in silence for twenty minutes or so with Georgine taking in the view of the country roadside. Marcello turned onto a winding trail diverging from the path they appeared to be taking to Jake's villa which was off the coast of Lazio, where he awaited them.

The scenery alternated between dusty paths, lush green fields and hilly vistas ripe with grapes of a nearby wine vineyard.

Marcello stopped the car and parked off road near a gathering of trees. Georgie waited as he climbed out and opened the trunk of the car. She opened her door and he looked up in surprise.

"Bella… wait there for me, I'll open it for you."

Georgie ignored him and stepped out, looking around. Marcello fished a couple of blankets, a basket, and a bottle of wine out of the trunk and gestured for her to follow him down a grassy slope to a shady clearing under a tree.

He opened one of his blankets, spreading it on the ground. Georgie sat down and signaled for him to hand her the basket.

She looked inside. Marcello sat on the other half of the blanket and helped empty the basket of its contents; various Italian dishes.

"It's still warm," Georgie said.

Penne pasta smothered in fresh vodka tomato sauce and parmesan, Italian pizza, fried ravioli appetizers, an array of garlic and butter glazed breads, olive salad and ricotta stuff mushrooms. For dessert, there was almond cake with Ricotta, dripping in chocolate and fruit.

"This is too much. I'm dancer. I'll have to

watch what I eat, but boy am I tempted!"

"In more ways than one, I hope…" Marcello said, with a lift of his brow. "It's not like the Italian food Americans prepare in your country, on the contrary our foods are not only appetizing, but very healthy."

"Are you sure?"

Marcello pinched a small piece of garlic loaf and tried to stuff it in her mouth – but Georgie grabbed his hand, took it away and fed herself a smaller piece.

"Whole grain. Not bad!" she exclaimed, rolling her eyes as if in a state of ecstasy.

She made a plate of pasta and greens, served with a roll on the side. Marcello poured them both a glass of wine.

"Where are we?" Georgie asked, looking around.

"We're at la Vigna di Giordano."

"Giordano? Like your last name…."

"Si, it's my family's vineyard."

"But you're a tour guide…."

"The touring company is my own business. My way, of getting away from my parents."

"Why?" she asked between bites.

"There's a girl. Our families are pressuring us. They want us to get married. But she loves my brother, Fredo."

"What's her name?"

"Rosalina."

"Do you love her?"

"No."

They ate in silence for a few minutes more and finished half a bottle of wine.

"So you're a dancer," Marcello said, rising to his feet. "Will you dance with me, Georgina?"

"I can't… no… I shouldn't."

"Because of your boyfriend, yes? A little dance never hurt anyone. It will pass the time, give us something to do until it's time to meet your boyfriend at his villa. Then I will take you to see how we make our wine, it will be an adventurous walk."

Marcello reached out, grabbing her hand as he pulled her to her feet, drawing her close until his hand was pressed against the small of her back.

They swayed to Marcello's tune, which he hummed against the back of her ear.

"I didn't see any of this on your brochure."

"It's only for special customers," he replied, trailing a kiss from her cheeks to her lips.

Georgie closed her eyes and thought of Jake. It was at that very moment, that she knew he was the only man she wanted to be with. She turned away, rebuffing Marcello's attempted kiss.

He laughed and spun her around, smiling as he rotated until he was standing behind her, arms wrapped around her waist, looking over her shoulder at the blanket.

"That wasn't so bad, was it?"

He let her go and gulped the rest of his wine down in one long swig. "You're a good woman."

Marcello put the remnants of their lunch back into the basket. Georgie helped. She folded the blankets and carried them back to the car.

Marcello took her for a two hour tour of the Giordano Vineyard. He then looked at his watch, and decided that they should be on their way.

Georgie fell asleep for the rest of the hour long ride. She awoke when the car met unpaved road again.

Marcello had turned and entered the driveway of a villa. The villa was built of white marble stone and rested on the edge of a cliff overlooking the lake. The air smelled of a combination of fresh water and baked bread. She wondered if there was a bakery nearby or if someone was baking inside of the house.

She looked up, and saw him gazing at her through the rear view mirror.

"Are you gonna marry Rosalina, Marcello?"

He parked the car in the rocky parking lot behind the villa and climbed out. He opened Georgie's door and took her hand within his.

"No..." he said, meeting her brown eyes. His lips rested over her knuckles and suddenly he kissed the back of her fingers.

"But I think a very special lady will find her way into my heart soon enough."

He gave her a very pointed look as he released her hand and walked around to the side of the car to shut the door.

Georgie stood beside him and waited for him to escort her inside. She reached for her luggage but Marcello grabbed it first. Their hands brushed together and Georgie quickly pulled away.

"Marcello? I have something to ask you."

"What is it?"

"I found your card in my hotel suite."

He gave her a roguish smile. "I saw you in the hotel lobby yesterday and told concierge to give you my card. On the other side I wrote that we should get together while you are visiting and to give me a call. I guess you weren't interested." He raised a brow. "Come with me," he said.

All she wanted to do was see Jake so she quickly followed Marcello into the house.

There to meet them was a housekeeper and a cook. The cook sat a basket full of fresh baked bread on the table as they walked in.

Georgie took in the view. The floors were a soft pink color that swirled into the white marble and the living room had a terrace that overlooked the lake.

"Hi, I'm Georgine."

She extended a hand to one of the housekeepers.

"Ciao, wel-come," the woman said with a

thick Italian accent. "My name is *Ro*-sa".

"Nice to meet you Rosa. And you are?"

The second housekeeper, a slender woman in her fifties, stepped forward. "Ciao, I'm Cilla, nice to meet you."

Her accent was not as difficult to understand.

"Pleasure to meet you as well," Georgie replied. "Is Jake around? Or is he away at work?"

It was a good thing they both spoke some English, as Georgie knew only one word in Italian.

"Mr. Lyggle is here."

Rosa gestured toward the door and Georgie turned around. Jake stood on the other side of the room, leaning against the door frame. His gaze drifted from Georgie and landed on Marcello's face. Jake wore a dark button down shirt, which had been rolled at the sleeves, and a pair of slacks. She could tell he had just come in from work. But so early in the day? It was only mid-afternoon.

She rushed to him, throwing her arms around his neck, not caring about Marcello or the housekeepers. Jake stumbled back.

She wrapped her arms around his shoulders and buried her face into the collar of his shirt. He smelled good, just as he always did. Jake's hand slipped to the small of her back. She turned around, embarrassed at realizing that every eye in the room was turned upon them.

"What are we doing here? You didn't tell me you were leaving the hotel. I was worried sick."

"Two reasons. I thought we could use some time apart... and I wanted to surprise you."

He gave Georgie a smile and she knew all was forgiven on both sides now.

"Well you certainly did that..."

Jake leaned forward and kissed her hungrily. Georgie wanted more, but with so many eyes watching she decided to save her kisses for later. She caught a glimpse of Marcello from the side of her eye, he watch them more intensely than the others.

"How was the tour? Did you see everything you wanted to see?" Jake asked.

"I took the long way to the villa. So she saw plenty of Rome and *all* it has to offer."

Marcello gave Georgie another pointed stare, which luckily, escaped Jake's notice.

"Good."

Jake met the man's stare.

"Did you send the Prefatturra Della Casa Pontifica?" he asked.

"Preffa-what? What is that?"

Georgie's gaze bounced back and forth between the two men. Marcello and Jake locked eyes.

"It's a letter requesting audience with the Pope," Jake answered without looking at her.

"You can do that?"

"Of course, I thought it was something you might want to do while we're in Rome."

"Sure, sounds wonderful. But what I really want to do is visit some of the basilicas, only I didn't want to see them without you. Marcello did offer to take me."

"Perhaps I might take you to St. Peter's basilica. We can visit St. Pietro's dome. It was designed by Michelangelo himself."

"We'll schedule something for tomorrow, Marcello. Thank you for giving Georgie a tour of the city."

"It was a pleasure meeting you," Marcello said.

They shook hands like perfect gentlemen but Marcello didn't so much as glance at Jake. His eyes were on Georgie. A strange discomforting feeling washed over her. Jake could not have missed that! She slipped an arm behind Jake's back and gave him a squeeze---she knew who she wanted to be with. No man was going to steal her heart away from her Jakey.

"Thanks again and nice to meet you Marcello," she said.

With that, Marcello was gone. Jake pulled Georgie by the hand and together they walked to the terrace. Jake stood behind her with his arms around her waist. They drank the cool summery air and watched as waves from the lake crashed against the bottom of the cliff.

Georgie felt Jake's breath against the side of her face as he leaned close to whisper into her ear. He nibbled her lobe and brushed his fingers along her right arm until his hand was on top of hers. She held onto the marble railing. His touch sent a jolt of electricity between her legs.

"I was starting to think you ran off with Marcello."

"It's not like I know my way around Rome. He could have taken any route he wanted and I wouldn't know the difference. "

"Yeah, well I don't like the way he looks at you."

"You're not jealous again are you?"
She wondered why he hired the man in the first place. Was it to watch their body language? To see if there was something between them?

"Should I be?"
There was something odd about the sound of his voice.

"I just met the man, Jake." She rubbed his hand, which rested over one of hers.

Jake kissed the nape of her neck. She turned to look at his face and kissed him back.

"So what are we doing today?" Georgie asked. "Any more surprises?"

"Seeing a tailor."

"For what?"

"To buy a dress. You need a new one to see the Pope."

"Why do I need a new dress? I still have clothes I haven't even worn yet. When are we going?"

"Tomorrow."

"I'm nervous."

"Don't be...it's not a private meeting. We'll hear the Pope with the rest of the crowd."

"Are you Catholic?"

"A devout Catholic as a matter of fact. Tomorrow we're going to confess our sins then... I have a surprise for you."

"But I'm not Catholic. I'm Baptist. There's a big difference between the two!"

He held her hand. "Don't worry, I love you anyway."

He closed his eyes when he kissed her on the lips.

"Just do this one thing for me, Georgie, and I promise to make it worth your while."

Never mind the fact that he was practically asking her to convert, Georgie was still in shock that Jake had used the "L" word. She didn't know what to say—how to respond. Had he said it in jest? Did he want her to say it too?

If the day's events had taught her anything, it was how quickly her world disintegrated when she thought her relationship with Jake was over.

"I love you too," Georgie replied.

She waited for her announcement to register but he said nothing, gazing over the balcony at the waves crashing below.

"What do you love about me, Georgie?"
He gave her a weird look. She could tell by the expression in his eyes that he was genuinely puzzled. She wanted then, to retract her words, to nudge him in the ribs with her elbow and tell him she was joking – she had gotten too serious too fast for their relationship, but decided the truth was always best whenever possible.

"I love your confidence…" she kissed him on the lips. "How handsome you are… I feel safe when I'm with you, and I enjoy your company, our conversations... and when we're alone, I feel like we're the only two people in the world, like nothing or no one else matters. I just love you. Do I need a reason why?"

He gazed at her face as if to ascertain her sincerity.

"I'm sorry-I shouldn't have said anything," Georgie said. Disappointment sank to her gut like a stone.

Jake turned and strode away from the terrace.

"Don't worry about it," he shrugged. "Don't forget to see the tailor today. Rosa will go with you."

That night, Georgie laid awake in bed and stared out of the window. She tried her best to shake off the embarrassment she felt. She was so depressed she couldn't even work up the strength to bemoan the fact that they hadn't made love. The last time was in a bathroom on the plane from Paris.

Jake made no mention of her confession the rest of the day. In fact, he made sure to avoid her until it was close to bedtime.

When he met her in the bedroom and saw her waiting for him on her side of the bed in the sexy lingerie she was wearing, he quickly went on a tangent about how tired he was then promptly went to sleep.

After one promise after another to go home, she felt she had finally worn out her welcome and decided to leave first thing after the address by the Pope – an opportunity she would probably never get again, so she was definitely going. Georgie knew if she told Jake she was leaving, out of kindness he would make an attempt to convince her to stay. After all, he did lure her away from the Pink Poodle to go away with him. There she might have had legitimate and loving relationship with Renard.

The next morning Georgie woke early, just as she had done to prep for her escape from the Pink Poodle. She showered then quietly went through all of the drawers and closets she had just settled her clothes into the night before, and packed them back into her suitcases.

When she was done, she left to get ready. She was standing in the bathroom in front of the mirror applying mascara to her eyes when she heard a knock.

Georgie opened the bathroom door wearing only a cream colored petticoat to go under the dress she picked out to wear on their trip to see the pope. They could end on friendly terms, depending on how Jake decided to handle the situation. She of course, had decided to bawl her eyes out on the flight back home, that was a given.

Georgie opened the door. Jake stood on other side rubbing sleep out of his eyes. He wore a plain white T-shirt and a pair of basketball shorts to bed. He had a five o'clock shadow. Even a disheveled, he was still sexiest man alive.

She brushed past him and walked to the closet, pulling out the lace embroidered cream colored dress the tailor fitted for her the day before.

She turned and caught a glimpse of Jake's face. He looked at her through a crack in the door, a wink in his eye as he closed it. Georgie heard the shower turn on.

She left and went to the kitchen where Rosa was making breakfast. She wasn't used to having meals cooked for her and for the first time was happy thinking about home where she would have some normalcy in her life again.

Georgie tried to make small talk with Rosa, which proved a difficult task. The woman's English was broken and difficult to understand... not that Georgie's Italian was any better.

Cilla joined them a few minutes later. They were able to have a conversation then.

To their surprise, Georgie sat in the kitchen and ate with the two women. It was unusual for an employer or a guest to eat with the "help".

They were a little apprehensive as if she had breached some social taboo, but was put at ease when she fetched her own food from the stove.

"So... does Jake visit here often?"

"Not very often," Cilla said.

"That's surprising. It's beautiful here. The view is breathtaking."

"Yes, I enjoy it very much."

"So when Jake isn't here do you get other renters?"

"Renters? Oh, no, we never have renters in Senor Lyggle's house. He wouldn't like it, though, it would give us something to do."

"Senor Lyggle's house? So Jake *lives* here?"

"Si. Sometimes," Rosa smiled.

"He likes you. Very much," Cilla replied.

Georgie bit her tongue. It took everything in her not to pour her heart out and to keep from asking how many women he often brought there. Knowing Jake, she was probably not the first.

The ladies chatted for a few minutes more about the property, Rosa's foods, and Jake's favorite meals as if Georgie would be the one cooking them. The thought made her smile. She barely cooked for herself.

They were just clearing their plates from the kitchen table when the door opened and Jake came strolling in.

"Good morning, ladies."

He looked around the room. He was dapper in a button down shirt and a pair of slacks with his hair gelled and brushed away from his cleanly shaved face.

He grabbed a roll from the table and bit into it.

"Is that what you're having for breakfast?" Georgie asked.

"I don't have time for breakfast today. You forgot to wake me up. We got forty minutes to get to St. Peter's."

"Oh crap."

Georgie looked at her watch. She grabbed her purse, quickly bade the women goodbye and followed Jake out the door. He drove them to the Vatican City, a small area less than a few blocks long. The Catholic Church ruled the Vatican as a religious monarchy, and as a separate state within Italy.

Georgie saw priests, monks, and various holy men traveling to and from its churches. There were throngs of visitors... some of them were tourists. Others were devout Catholics on pilgrimages.

Jake held her hand as they walked. She was in awe. St. Peter's was so grand it eclipsed the sky. There were sixteen Corinthian styled columns at the top of the steps before the entrance and 'Basilica Sancti Petri' written in Latin just above it. Large angelic statues of the saints overlooked the grounds like beautiful gargoyles.

The interior was even more impressive. She couldn't believe she was standing in a four hundred year-old architectural triumph with its arched ceilings, paintings, bronze and gold statues and decorations perfected down to the minutest detail. But most of all, she was in awe that Jake had cared enough to take her. Without him she would never have had an opportunity to visit such a beautiful and holy place. It just made her appreciate their time together even more for however long it was going to last.

After a lengthy tour of the church, and St. Pietro's dome, Jake was more affectionate than ever, kissing her hand and wrapping his arms around her shoulders whenever they stopped.

Jake didn't tell her that the Pope would be there, praying at the altar of St. Peter's burial ground.

The venerable religious leader addressed the crowd but the speech and mass was cut short. The Pope was out of sorts and looked weary. There was a rumor circulating that the Pope was ill.

Georgie was glad when they left and sat

down at a nearby restaurant in Rome for lunch.

Jake held her hand across the table. He was smiling more than she'd seen him smile in weeks.

"I know I've been working a lot. But I have a surprise for you. I'll make it up to you babe, I promise."

He leaned across the table and kissed her. She tried to look casual.

"There's nothing to be sorry about. You said it was a business trip. I can always go home when I'm tired of it."

"Hell, not that again."

"It's not a big deal, Jake. You'll see me in Connecticut, right?"

"I don't want to see you in Connecticut, I want to see you here. Dammit, I rarely visit Connecticut."

"I thought you had a house in Greenwich?"

"I do, I grew up there. You don't' get it do you? I don't want you to leave. I need to have you with me."

"You're the one who doesn't get it. I'm done with the Pink Poodle, I'm done with my trip through Europe. Why do you want me to stay? What do you want?"

"I want you to rely on me."

"I have a life. I can't stick around and live yours. I have a family. If you want to see me again you'll have to visit me at home. I appreciate everything you've done. But…"

Jake silenced her with a hand over her lips.

"Today is supposed to be special and I don't want to argue. Let's talk about it tonight."

Jake threw his fork on top of his plate. "You done yet?"

A few minutes later they were in the car driving through Rome when all Georgie wanted to do was kick her heels off and get back to the villa.

"Jake, I'm tired. Let's go back to the villa. You can share the surprise with me tomorrow."

"I can't," he smiled, turning to look at her briefly. "We have to do it today."

"Do what?"

She had yet to tell him that she had already booked a flight home and that they were quickly approaching the time she was to set out for the airport. The way she planned it, she would arrive in the States early morning just before dawn when traffic was light.

Georgie could tell they were far away from the villa by how long they had been driving and the fact that the scenery changed from that of a busy metropolitan city to rural countryside. She decided that they were somewhere on the outskirts of Rome.

Jake drove to a vacant space at the bottom of a hill. At the top was a small church with a winding path that led to its courtyard and two front doors.

They got out of the car.

After complaining about her feet again, Jake whipped Georgie into his arms and carried her up. Her shoes fell from her feet and rolled down the steep hill toward the car.

"Of all the churches in Rome! What's so special about this place?"

"You'll see…" Jake replied.

They reached the top. In the courtyard outside of the church was a fountain and at its center was a statue of one of the Saints. Georgie wasn't sure of which one it was and didn't ask. Water poured from flutes on all sides.

Jake gestured for her to sit on the stone surround. "It's a small church but the garden is better than any of the ones we'll see at other churches in Rome."

"Where are we?"

"Saint Theresa. I wanted to take you for a walk around the garden. I heard there were over a hundred thousand flowers there. It's peaceful here. I visit whenever I'm in Rome. There's a bridge around the bend and a gazebo."

Georgie turned and looked behind them. She could see the garden and finely sculpted bushes from where they sat.

"But I want to talk about something else."

He took her hand in his.

"I hired a private detective. He did a background check on you."

"Why on earth would you do that? What in the hell did you think, I was some type of criminal?"

She tried to pull her hand away but Jake

held firm. Georgie's heart thumped wildly in her chest.

"Jeez, calm down. I didn't mean anything by it, Georgie. I had to prove you've never been married before."

"If you wanted to know whether or not I've been married before you could have asked!"

"You don't understand... that's not what I think. I had to prove it to the church. It's a requirement for couples who get married in Italy."

"What does that have to do with us?"

He gave her a stupid look.

"I'm asking you to marry me, Georgine."

Jake went into his pocket and showed Georgie a fuzzy pink ring box. He held it before her and opened it but Georgie couldn't bring herself to look at the sparkling diamond. Her heart was aflutter. Jake dropped to his knee and repeated the question...

"Will you marry me?"

A proposal was the last thing Georgie expected.

She sat on the stone surround with

trembling hands clasped over her mouth, tears swelling in her eyes.

"I want to…"

"If you want to then say yes."

"We hardly know each other."

"So."

"You can't be serious about this!"

"I'm serious about you and that's all that matters. I love you, Georgie."

She pulled him to her and held him tight.

"I'm scared. We can't do this."

"You told me you felt safe when you were with me so what are you afraid of now?"

If there was anything to get off of her chest, now was the time….

"When I told you I loved you, you were angry with me. You don't talk to me that much, you work a lot, you're jealous and we haven't made love since we've been here. We've known each other for less than two months. I need to make sure I'm doing the right thing regardless of how I feel about you."

"I was afraid you might say that. Georgie, I told you the moment I laid eyes on you I knew what I wanted."

"That's fine, but how long till the novelty wears off? What happens to me then?"

"You're not a novelty. I love you more than life itself. I'm sorry I didn't respond the other night when you said you loved me. I was overwhelmed and I felt insecure. You're too good for me. I know I don't deserve you."

She kissed him on the lips.

"That's not true, I meant every word. I love you too."

"If you love me, then marry me."

He waited for her to answer. Georgie looked into his eyes and knew he was serious. What would her father say?

"Yes... I-I'll marry you, Jake."

He pulled her into his arms and kissed her again. It wasn't a flat affectionless kiss like the others he'd given her since their arrival, but deep and passionate.

Jake stood and pulled Georgie by the hand.

"Where are we going?"

"To the church," he answered.

"I thought we were going for a walk around the garden?"

"Yeah, we'll do that after."

"After what?"

"After you change clothes."

"I didn't bring a change of clothes. What do I need them for?"

"I sent a change of clothes to the church this morning."

"Goodness Jake! For what? Please tell me what's going on."

Georgie was at a loss. She stood helplessly before the church doors waiting for him to answer.

"I told you I had a surprise for you."

"Jake please tell me what you're up to now. I don't think my heart can take any more surprises."

"Isn't it obvious?"

"What?" she shrieked.

"I said, I love you. Now get inside," he smiled.

He opened the church doors. Inside was quiet, empty and decorated with flowers. It smelled like church. Funny how all churches had that same smell.

"Let's get married today."

Georgie turned and paced toward the door

but Jake was on her heels. He grabbed her by the arm and drew her back inside. This was too ridiculous to believe.

"I feel faint! This is happening too fast!"

"Don't get cold feet on me. You said you would marry me, so why not marry me now? What's the difference between today or two years?"

"We'd know each other better, we'd know we're doing the right thing."

"My gut is telling me this is the right thing."

He was smiling. She knew he was teasing her.

"You're putting me under so much pressure! This is crazy, Jake. We can't do this *now*. What if we change our minds?"

He sat her in one of the pews and kneeled before her again.

"I know I'm pushy but I promise to explain everything as soon as we get back to the villa."

"What is it? Do you need a green card? I don't understand."

Jake laughed.

"I love you. I want to spend the rest of my

life with you. I want to have children, I want to have everything with you. I'm begging you Georgie. Let's get married! I made all the arrangements, you don't need to do a thing."

He pulled her by the arm and led her to a room at the back of the church.

Rosa and Cilla was waiting for her there with a wedding dress.

"I'm not supposed to see it," he said, turning his back. "So I won't look. Cilla and Rosa helped. I hired a photographer to take pictures and Father Brioni is waiting for us."

Georgie stared at Cilla and Rosa in awe. Jake had truly thought of everything. Everything but asking her first!

Still, the gesture was sweet and even a little romantic despite his heavy handed overtures.

She left Jake standing outside the door and got dressed. She loved Jake, so why shouldn't she marry him? He was handsome, romantic, a good lover, when they did make love, awesome company when he lent her his time, but most importantly, he loved her too. Unconditionally. It didn't matter if she was rich or poor, or whether she worked in corporate America or a stinking burlesque. He loved her enough to go through the trouble of marrying her when he could have any woman he wanted.

The wedding dress Rosa and Cilla picked out was a crushed cream colored corset ball gown.

"It's a gorgeous dress," Rosa said.

They stood beside the wedding gown, excited as they waited for Georgie to put it on.

"Go, put it on!" Cilla gushed.

Georgie peeled out of her clothes and slid into the undergarments that went with her gown.

"How did you guess my size?"

"When you go to tailor, they tell us," Cilla replied.

When Georgie was done, they went to the bathroom and styled her hair, pinning it into a bun at the top of her head. They stuck little hair pins with pearls beaded onto them as decoration.

Using a small thin comb they attached the veil as the finishing touch. Georgie washed her face then reapplied her makeup using

151 Infatuation by E. Hughes

items she carried around in her purse.

Rosa gave her a box with a pair of pearl earrings and matching necklace inside.

She fastened it around her neck.

"You look beautiful…"

"Thank you, Cilla."

Georgie stared in the mirror at her reflection. She was the perfect bride. It was no one's guess how abruptly the wedding descended upon her.

She followed Cilla and Rosa outside to the garden where a small gathering of chairs were assembled. In the first few rows sat four guys. All of them people she had met before. Jake stood with Father Brioni under the gazebo which had been decorated with a collection of flowers. Cilla and Rosa sat down.

Georgie waited, unsure as to whether or not she should approach.

Jake nodded and Chris left his seat to stand by Georgie's side.

"I'll walk you down the aisle," he said with a smile.

All she could think about was how her father was going to kill her.

"About time you guys made it official."

Georgie turned and looked at Chris as a nun with a viola began to play the wedding song.

"About time?"

"Jake told us you were getting married. That's why we flew to France."

"You must be mistaken."

He gave her a look like she was the crazy one.

Georgie turned her gaze to Jake. What did Chris mean? How is it possible that he flew to France for a wedding before she and Jake were even a couple? Or had Jake planned to marry someone else? There were things about Jake that just didn't seem to add up. Much as she tried to ignore the red flags, citing paranoia as a reason not to trust him, this new revelation gave her pause. Was he on the rebound?

Was there an ulterior motive? Something wasn't right.

Chris linked his arms into hers and they made their way down the aisle. Jake's eyes were transfixed on Georgie's face as she approached. And yet, she could hardly bring herself to meet his eyes.

She stood before him as the music quieted and dismissed her doubt as pre-wedding jitters. She wanted to call the whole thing off but couldn't bring herself to disappoint the man she loved. He looked so happy.

Father Brioni introduced himself, gave them instructions and recited the vows... words she'd heard before at other weddings only this version was uniquely Catholic.

"Do you take Jake Lyggle... for better or worse, for richer or poorer..." the priest continued.

A full thirty seconds later, Georgie answered. "I will."

Father Brioni recited the same vows to Jake, who barely allowed the priest to finish before he replied, "I will."

Soon Georgie's new husband was lifting the veil from her face and kissing her on the lips.

They had a small celebration at a nearby Italian restaurant. Jake and Georgie had eyes for no one but each other. They danced until the restaurant was empty.

"This is perfect," Jake said.

"Almost perfect. I wish my parents were here."

"We'll renew our vows when we get to the States. You can hire a wedding planner or do it all yourself this time. The anguish of planning a wedding is a rite of passage. "

"Makes the outcome that much sweeter, doesn't it? Like when a pregnant woman goes through childbirth. The pain is indescribable. Yet when she holds her newborn baby in her arms for the first time it's all but forgotten. The same goes for a wedding!"

"Are you thinking about a baby?" he smiled.

Georgie frowned. "Get pregnant? Not if my life depended on it. Maybe in a few years. I want you all to myself. "

There was also her career to think about. She pulled him close.

"What about you?"

"I'd like a son one day. Maybe two."

"It's not like you have a choice in the matter! What if we have a daughter?"

Jake spun her around and dipped her back.

"I'd love her just the same. But a son I would worry less about. I'd have to hire a security guard to watch over my girls."

"What about a son and a daughter?"

"It would be perfect. Just like everything else."

"Would you consider adoption?"

"It depends on the situation. Why?"

"Just wondering."

She lowered her eyes. They left the dance floor and went back to their table.

Paul, Steve, Chris, and Roberto were also there. They toasted the event, teased and ridiculed each other, drank wine, and ate cake. Soon, the restaurant was closing and it was time to go home.

"I gotta get going guys. The old lady could pop any day now," Steve said.

"Your wife is having a baby and you flew all the way to Italy to go to our wedding?" Georgie asked.

"It was important to Jake. Don't worry, the baby's due in a month. I'll take the next flight moving tonight," he said, straightening his tie. Steve stumbled away from the table, knocking a glass over.

"I'll get him back to the hotel, Chris said.

Roberto, Paul, Georgie and Jake separated in the parking lot.

Jake was so sloppy drunk, Georgie had to beg him for directions to the villa but eventually stopped at a hotel less than a mile away from the restaurant.

She wasn't exactly sober herself and couldn't get used to driving on the right side of the car.

They left the car and Jake leaned on her shoulder as they walked inside. His body felt like it weighed a ton.

Georgie went to the front desk and while she couldn't' speak a word of Italian she managed to not only get a room...but a nice one, using money left over from her plane ticket. It didn't take a genius to guess that they wanted the honeymoon suite and lucky for them, there was one available.

The room had a king size bed, a terrace, a living room, kitchen and a sauna.

Georgie dragged Jake to the bedroom. He stumbled across the floor and collapsed on top of the bed in his tuxedo dizzily.

She pulled his shoes off then collapsed

beside him. Her wedding night wasn't quite what she expected, but she was too tired to give a damn.

"I screwed up again," he grumbled drunkenly.

"You have the rest of your life to make it up to me."

Georgie laughed and softly kissed the side of his face.

"I'll order some coffee," she said.

She called the front desk and managed to place an order. Room service arrived thirty minutes later, but Jake was still asleep.

She unbuttoned his tuxedo jacket, unraveled his tie to keep him from choking to death should he decide to puke, and shook him awake.

Jake woke up and grumbled incoherently before graciously sipping the piping hot java. A few minutes later he turned and found Georgie beside him, unconscious, still in her wedding dress.

Hours rolled by and at four in the morning, just before dawn, Georgie opened her eyes. She felt something soft and moist against her face. Her first instinct was to swat whatever it was away. But then, she realized Jake was kissing her.

His touch made her feel breathless.

He nuzzled the side of her neck with his mouth and slowly unzipped the back of her dress. He was shirtless and laying on his side. Her hands traveled down his muscular abs, softly and seductively.

He moved the veil from her hair, tossed it on the floor and climbed over her body. Georgie put her foot against his chest. Jake smiled and slid her garter off. He flung it across the room as she wiggled out of her dress.

After unclasping the hooks on the bustier she wore beneath it, he descended upon her.

"What took you so long?" Georgie asked.

They consumed each other with hot passionate kisses.

"I told you I was devoutly Catholic. I know we made love before, but I wanted to make things official before we did it again. It took every ounce of strength in my body to turn you away night after night. I'm sorry…"

He kissed her forehead.

"Why didn't you tell me?"

"Because I would have given in if you tried to talk me out of it."

"I love you," Georgie said.

"I love you too."

CHAPTER EIGHT

Jake and Georgie flew back to the States by private jet two weeks after the wedding. The honeymoon was officially over and Jake was worried.

The family attorneys were going to hit the roof about his marrying without a prenup. Jake decided, he would yet again have to remind them that they worked for him and not the other way around. He could marry whoever the hell he wanted, especially a woman he considered to be his soul mate.

He knew there were people in his inner circle who would refuse to accept her. And likewise, there would be members of her inner circle who would refuse to accept him. Georgie had yet to tell her parents about the wedding. By her account, her father was a strict traditional man who wouldn't take kindly to Jake marrying her without soliciting his permission first. In fact, her father was notoriously overprotective of his eldest daughter.

Henderson, Jake's driver, met them at the airport in a black Mercedes Benz. He drove them to an upscale Greenwich neighborhood to the Lyggle family estate, an hour long drive away from the private airport.

Georgie gripped Jake's hand as they approached the house, which was perched at the top of a hill above all the neighboring homes. The gates, which looked like two harps that had been pushed together separated as the car proceeded onto the cobbled driveway.

Georgie muttered "I love you" to Jake as the car rolled at a slow five miles per hour to the door. The smile on her face overflowed with sweetness and love.

Jake replied with equal sincerity and they kissed as the car parked in front of the house. He looked up and caught Henderson watching them through the rear view mirror. They got out of the car.

"Henderson, this is Georgine, my new wife," Jake said.

"Wow, congratulations," Henderson replied. There was a cheerful pitch to his voice and a look of complete surprise on his face.

"Nice to meet ya Henderson," Georgie said.

She bent down to grab her shoulder bag and Jake pinched her back side. Georgie turned and slapped him across the arm.

He led her into the house and pointed out the different rooms when they got inside.

"This place is huge," Georgie said. "But a little dark. Maybe some new curtains would help. The drapes are a little outdated."

"I have the furniture and drapes refurbished every few years. My great grandmother, Nancy Lyggle decorated this house."

"You don't think it's a little old fashioned?"

"The house was decorated in the 1920s just before she died. It's just the way she left it."

"You mean to tell me this furniture has been here more than eighty years? How old was your great grandmother when she passed away?"

"She was in her thirties. My grandfather was only ten years-old when she died."

Jake looked away.

"What happened?"

"I'd rather not talk about it, Georgie."

"I'm sorry," she said.

Jake kissed her on cheek. "Don't' worry about it."

He left Georgie at the foot of the stairs with a confused expression on her face. She looked up and gazed at the chandelier. It creaked as if it might fall. The house was old and the chandelier made strange noises, but Jake knew it was secure.

Georgie followed him upstairs.

Jake gave her a tour of the bedroom, the adjoining bathroom and closets. Georgie opened her suitcases which sat near the door. But Jake told her to leave it. The maid would unpack her clothes and put them away.

He knew it would take a while before Georgie got used to the idea of having a maid. Let alone a maid who would go through her personal belongings.

"So who lives here?" she asked.

"We do."

"Anyone else?"

"Rosetta and my assistant, Jim."

"I'm not used to living with strangers, Jake."

He pulled her to him and pressed his body against hers. There was a worried expression on Georgie's face.

"We're the only two people in the world, remember? I've been dreaming about this for a long time."

She closed her eyes as he kissed her on the lips and unbuttoned her blouse.

"Stop."

"Why?"

"You have to meet my parents."

"Let's do it tomorrow."

"Jake, they're probably worried sick by now. I won't break the news over the phone. I'm not that cruel. Let's go downstairs, get in the car and drive to Cornwall."

Jake groaned.

Georgie pulled him by the lapels and kissed him.

CHAPTER NINE

The drive to Cornwall was more than an hour and a half long because of heavy midday traffic. Jake was exhausted after their flight from Europe and wanted to rest. But Georgie was resolved on going to see her parents. Jake mentally prepared himself for the drama.

They took Cty PD 89 for part of the drive. In fact, he intentionally took that route to gauge a reaction from Georgie. Not very scenic, but there were a few old houses, shacks, and slaughter houses nearby. He slowed down, taking it all in.

"Why are you stopping here?" Georgie complained, clutching his upper arm. "I don't like it here. Take the main highway…" she demanded, tightening her lips.

The drive to her parents house was over an hour away and not long after, they had arrived.

The house was in the heart of Cornwall just over a windmill bridge and part of a nearby apple grove of which her father was the caregiver. Georgie told Jake that her father bought the land after her parents retired, just before her graduation from high school.

The Louvelles lived in a typical country house. It had large scenic windows and a view of the countryside and a wrap-around porch trimmed with rose bushes. It was a cool windy day. The shutters of the old house rattled and the screen door blew open and closed in the breeze.

Jake sat in a rocking chair on her parent's porch as Georgie pushed their unlocked door open and walked inside.

"Georgie?" a female voice called in surprise. "Louis! Oh dear Lord, Georgie's home!"

"Hey mom," Georgie said.

The door closed behind her, leaving Jake outside before he could properly stand and introduce himself to her mother. But the window was open. He could hear them loud and clear as they stood in the kitchen and talked.

"Where on earth have you been? We

thought you were dead! We called the café, they told us you abandoned the show. We called the Embassy, and they said they haven't heard from you since the day you arrived. We called every airline we could possibly think of, but they wouldn't give us information."

"I quit my job at *Le Caniche Rose* and went to Italy."

"Italy! What on earth were you doing in Italy? You couldn't call? Your father is so upset. And what about Olivia and Oliver?"

Jake wondered who Olivia and Oliver were.

Georgie sighed. "I'm sorry."

"All of us were worried sick."

"I had a terrible time in Paris at first, but I was determined to work my way out of it. I got myself into that mess and I was going to get myself out. Then something wonderful happened and next thing you know, I was in Italy!"

"What kind of *wonderful* are you talking about?"

"So you finally decided to show up?" a voice interrupted. "Your mother and I were worried sick."

Jake figured it was probably her father speaking.

"I'm sorry dad. I didn't mean to scare you or upset Olivia and Oliver. I went to Italy."

"I thought we agreed that you were going to France?"

"Agreed? Jeez, dad. What am I? A five year-old?" she rolled her eyes.

"You're right. We're flying off the handle," her mother said, taking a deep breath.

"How was your trip?"

"You were right, dad. Lucky lied about *Le Caniche Rose*. Turns out, it was a seedy run down café in the Red Light District."

"I know," the father said. "Your mother and I looked it up on the internet. The place was a real shit hole."

"...So I went to Italy."

"What were you doing in Italy?" her mother asked.

Georgie took a deep breath.

"Promise you won't overreact."

"Brace yourself Irma. You know what happened the last time we heard those words."

"Dad… *please*."

"What is it?" Irma replied.

"I'm married."

She showed them her ring hand as she backed toward the door. Jake stood as the screen door swung open and Georgie stepped out.

"This is my new husband, Jake Lyggle."

Georgie's parents appeared in the doorway behind her - slack jawed.

"M-M-arried?" her father grumbled.

"Jake, this is my father Louis Louvelle. This is my mother… Irma."

"Nice to meet you," Jake said, extending a hand.

Louis stared at first then brusquely gripped his hand.

"No need to stand outside for the entire world to see. Come on in."

"Thank you," Jake replied.

They stood in the kitchen. Louis looked him up and down.

"I saw you in the paper last week. The article said something about getting married."

"You saw Jake in the paper?" Georgie

asked.

Louis shot her an angry look. "I have nothing to say to you right now."

Irma grabbed her husband by the arm. "It's her life. She has a right to get married if she wants."

"To him? I-I'm trying to figure this out. Just how did the two of you meet in France of all places? I wouldn't be surprised if they planned the whole thing from the beginning."

He cocked his head to the side and stared at Jake and Georgie.

Louis was tall, dark and imposing with a mean stare and a sharp baritone voice. The mother was petite with salt and pepper hair and a gentle face that looked a lot like Georgie's. Jake could tell the woman was probably as beautiful as her daughter at one time. In fact, she was still a very pretty woman.

"Don't worry about him," Irma said. "He'll come around. You kids have a seat at the table and have some dinner."

Jake reluctantly sat.

Louis' impact on Georgie was sharp. Her

hands were shaking and her shoulders were trembling. She couldn't look him in the face. But the man wasn't looking at his daughter. His eyes burned incisions through Jake.

Irma cluttered around the kitchen moving plates from the cabinet to the table. Georgie helped. They were standing near the stove stirring sauce when a young woman who looked to be in her early twenties with a thin resemblance to Georgie came bustling in with two noisy children.

"Hey, Georgie!" the young woman called.

She met her sister at the stove and gave her a hug. The two children, Olivia and Oliver followed.

"Hey you!" Georgie exclaimed. She pulled the kids into her arms and kissed them on their foreheads. "I missed you."

"We missed you too," the boy answered.

The little girl Olivia laid her head on Georgie's chest as she hugged her.

"Are you moving in with us again?" Oliver asked.

"No, but I'm just an hour away. You can visit any time you want. For as long as you want."

Georgie stole a look at her mother and father.

"Well, it's about time you came back. Where in the hell have you been?" the sister asked.

"Watch it. You're not too old to get your mouth washed out with soap," Irma chided.

Georgie smacked her lips. "In Italy. I got married."

The young woman opened her mouth wide with shock. "You got what!"

"Married, as a matter of fact. Jake, this is my sister, Anne."

"Oh, hello! So you're the big pink elephant in the room. Nice to meet ya. I was wondering why everybody was all tense and everything."

Georgie rolled her eyes.

"The two little ones are Olivia and Oliver," Georgie continued.

"And who are they?" Jake asked.

"Her brother and sister," Louis interrupted.

He gave Jake and Georgie a curious look. Irma stopped stirring the sauce in her pot and was looking at them.

Jake noticed the kids looked nothing like Georgie's parents.

"Wow," Anne said. "Married? I think I need a drink."

She shook her head.

"By the way, I've seen you before. In the newspaper. Aren't you...?"

"Jake Lyggle."

Anne gave Georgie a look of utter astonishment then sat at the table across from her new brother-in-law. "Where did you guys meet?"

"In France, at the café."

"Wow, Georgie, that place was a real dump. We looked it up on the internet."

Georgie looked over her shoulder at Anne and rolled her eyes. "I know. I can't say I regret working there. If not, I never would have met my Jake."

She looked at him and smiled.

Louis and Irma exchanged bewildered looks but Georgie seemed completely oblivious as she set the table.

A few minutes later everyone took turns washing their hands at the sink then sat down to eat. Irma and Georgie served the plates. Homemade lasagna, broiled chicken, salad, bread rolls, soup, and lemonade.

Georgie stared back and forth at Jake and her father while Louis took bites of his food and quietly stared at Georgie, Jake, Olivia and Oliver who all sat beside each other. The longer he stared, the angrier he looked.

Irma rubbed his shoulder every few minutes as if to calm him down.

"So, what do you for a living?" Anne asked. "Your family owned a lot of businesses right?"

"Yeah."

Jake slurped soup from his spoon.

"You must be loaded."

"Anne!" Georgie wailed. "It's rude to talk about money."

"It's rude for rich people, but I'm not rich so what do I care?"

Irma bit her lip and signaled with her eyes to get Anne's attention, but the young woman refused to look.

"How's the job?" Georgie interrupted.

"Boring."

Anne cut into her lasagna. "Did you guys take wedding pictures?"

"Actually we did. I made copies for everybody. Don't worry, we're getting married again. I want Olivia and Oliver to be a part of the ceremony, of course…"

"Can we see the pictures?" Olivia asked.

"Sure…"

Georgie opened her wallet and flipped through some of her wedding photos. The family leaned toward Olivia for a better look.

"Nice…but how was the honeymoon?" Anne wriggled her brows.

Louis dropped his spoon on the table and glared at Jake.

"May I have a word with you outside?"

Jake knew the family would be surprised by the marriage, but was hoping, not so contentious. Irma wiped tears from her eyes and Louis looked ready to rip Jake in half.

"Daddy? Is everything okay?"

"Stay here. I need to have a talk with Jake. Man to man."

"Dad, don't do anything crazy!" Anne called.

Louis grabbed his hat.

Georgie turned in her seat as the two men walked toward the door. Jake gave her a pointed stare. "We're going for a walk. I'll be right back."

Louis scoffed as they opened the door and walked out.

Jake and Louis descended the porch steps and walked across the field toward the apple grove in total silence. For the first time in a long time, Jake was actually nervous. He knew what the old man was angry about and now it was time to hash it all out.

When they were far away from the house, away from where anyone might hear them, Louis stopped. There was an empty basket near a tree. The family probably used it to carry apples.

"You just couldn't' stay away from her, could you?"

Jake looked over his shoulder toward the house. Georgie had stepped out onto the porch, searching for them in the distance.

"I don't know what you're talking about."

"I *know* who you are."

Jake narrowed his eyes.

"I told you to stay away from my daughter."

"I love Georgie. I would never do anything

to hurt her."

"Then why did you do it? Why come back?"

"Because I love her."

Louis walked toward the tree, bent down and put a fallen apple into the basket.

"You're not in love with my daughter. You're *infatuated*. After all this time you're still pining and *lusting* after her."

He turned and strode toward Jake again like he wanted to hit him.

"We still don't know what you did to her that night."

"Ask her yourself. She'll tell you, I didn't do anything to hurt her."

"How can I ask Georgine about something she doesn't even remember? You rich little shit, you think you can have anything you want, don't you? And the one thing you couldn't have, you just had to take. Not once, but twice."

"It wasn't like that. What Georgie and I have is special. Why would I marry someone I didn't love, honor or respect? Why would I give her my family's name?"

"Damn your family name! Let tell you

something, boy. If it wasn't for the fact that you married Georgie, showing your face around here would look real bad right now. In fact, I would have taken my rifle and shot you clean off of my property. But Georgie's happier than I've ever seen her, and I won't take that away. For my daughter's sake, I'm gonna give you a chance to explain yourself."

"Just hear me out," Jake said. The last thing he wanted to do was hurt his wife by getting into a tussle with her father. But he was just about run out of patience.

Louis folded both arms across his chest and waited.

****

The first time I saw Georgie I was in the eighth grade. I was a student at All Savior's. I lived in the boarding rooms away from my family and parents. Georgie had just transferred from a school in New York. We all knew she was an actress on that television show, so she made friends fast. I had the biggest crush on her. I told all of my friends that I was going to marry her one day.

I used to write Georgie love letters and slip them into the vents of her locker at school. She would get them then read them aloud to her friends then promptly toss them in the trash. I got angry after a while about the rejection. So I reacted the only way I knew how.

I bullied her... knocked her books from her hands, tipped her tray over at lunch, chased her home after school. We fought constantly and she hated my guts. Said I was the ugliest boy she had ever seen. And that just made me angrier because she wounded my ego, which was already fragile because of her.

One day, I was waiting outside on your lawn for Georgie to come out of the house. It was morning and I was going ask if my friend Paul Cutter and I could walk her to school, you know, make amends... she opened the door and the cat ran out. It was hit by a school bus. She started screaming so I ran. I never bothered her again after that. I knew she thought I was the one who did it. But the cat saw a squirrel and chased it into the street. A few months later I moved away and went to school in England where my father's new office was located....

When I was nineteen, he finally gave me permission to move back to the States. I transferred from Oxford to All Savior's College. That's when I saw her again. She was a still a student at All Savior's High School which was right across campus. I stayed clear of your daughter. I didn't harass her. I matured. One thing I did know was that I thought about her all the time when I was in England. I was happy to see her. But I didn't have the nerve to talk to her again.

Jake took a deep breath.

One night I was driving on Cty Pd 89, a rural stretch of road about five or six miles from the school when I saw a car on the side of road. I'd seen the car before and I knew it was Georgie's. I figured it was a flat tire or something.

I still had the biggest crush on her and thought it would be a good time to make up. So I pulled over just down the road and walked to her car. When I got there I saw her inside. She rolled the window down.

"Hey! You got a cell phone? I'm stranded but I can't get service on mine all the way out here in the boondocks."

Then taking a longer look at my face, she said, "Don't I know you?"

"From school. I went to All Savior's."

She breathed a sigh of relief.

"Oh cool. I'm Georgie."

"I hesitated to tell her who I really was. She didn't fully recognize me so I introduced myself as Jake."

"Nice to meet ya," she beamed "So, your cell phone working or what? I got a busted tire. There's a mechanic down the road...but he's closed."

"I can call someone for you," I offered.

I searched my pockets for my phone then flipped it open... 'Out of range' flashed on the led screen. "Shit."

"Oh damn. No service?"

"It's searching. Give it a minute or two. Otherwise, I can put your tire on for you."

"Can you really? Wow, you don't look like the kind of guy who'd know anything about fixing a car."

"Really? What kind of guy do I look like?"

"Like the sophisticated type...the kind of guy who wouldn't get his hands dirty."

I smiled and leaned against her car. I'd never been so happy to fix a spare tire in my life.

"Amazing what guys will do for a beautiful girl," I guess.

She got out of the car.

"Sorry I didn't get out before. It's the middle of the night, deserted road, handsome sophisticated mechanic."

She smiled.

"Right. Can't be too careful. Open the trunk."

"You won't chop me up and stuff me in it will you? I'm a little scared," she joked.

"Not until I fix the car," I quipped. "*Then* you go in the trunk."

"That is not at all funny," Georgie chided, hands on her hips.

With the headlights from my car shining on my face, she took a closer look.

"You know, I recognize you now. You're..." then sighing in disgust, she pulled her heels off. "You're Jughead. Aren't you?"

I shrugged. "That's what they called me."

"Figures. Only a guy like you would make a joke like that. Kill any cats lately? You know what they say, anybody who would kill a harmless animal is perfectly capable of hurting a human being."

Georgie stormed away from the car and walked toward the side of the road. "You know, never mind about the tire. There's a house on the other side of the ditch. I'll knock on the door and ask for help."

She ran so quickly I didn't get a chance to object. I hurried away from her open trunk and tried to find her in the distance, calling her name. But no answer. So I jumped into the ditch and followed.

I didn't' see Georgie, but a little further away there was a storage shed. At the time I didn't know what it was, exactly, but I knew it wasn't a house. Georgie was mistaken if she believed there was someone inside who could help her.

I walked about a half block. The shed wasn't as small as it looked from afar but the exterior was steel and cold to touch. Inside, I heard a voice echoing out to me, so I pulled this long steel bolt away from its lock and opened the door. It was pitch black in there. I couldn't see a thing so I went in and was about to call Georgie by name when suddenly, the door shut behind me. I was locked in.

Then I heard a whimpering in the darkness.

"Are you okay?" I asked.

"No…" she answered.

"Don't worry, I'll get us out."

I kicked the door over and over again to no avail. Then I remembered the bolt I unlocked to get in and realized kicking the door was useless.

"Where are you?"

"Over here…"

I followed the sound of her voice to the other side of the room. Then reaching out, I touched her hand.

She was trembling. The shed was cold. Freezing in fact. But my adrenaline was pumping so I didn't feel it at first. I sat beside her and snuggled close.

"Our cars are parked on the side of the road. Somebody is bound to find us.

We gotta stick together to keep from

freezing to death."

It was March and probably around zero degrees outside and Georgie wasn't wearing a coat. I worried that we'd freeze to death if we didn't get out soon.

I took my shoes off, gave her my socks, and offered to sit on her legs to warm them again. They were like blocks of ice. Then I gave her my coat.

I got up, stood in the center of the room and looked up. I must have stood there for a while, analyzing the situation and hoping there was a light switch up there, or maybe something on the wall near the door. Finding neither, I sat beside her again.

"Great. We're going to die and it's your fault."

"What? How is it *my* fault? You're the one who ran in here."

"If you hadn't scared me to death with that stupid joke of yours…"

"Get real. You didn't really think I'd stuff you in the trunk did you?"

"You killed my cat. So why not?"

"I didn't kill your cat. You were standing

in your doorway when she ran out and got hit by a car."

"I don't remember seeing Misty get hit by car!"

I could hear the sound of Georgie's hands rubbing up and down on her arms to generate heat. Then her teeth began to chatter. She'd been in the shed a few minutes longer than I had and was wearing a thin dress. I wore pants, an undershirt, over shirt, vest, and a jacket, which I'd worn to a party at the house of one of my father's clients. Georgie was grossly underdressed. But at least she had my coat.

"Why do you hate me so much?"

"How else am I supposed to feel about the jerk who bullied me and made my childhood a living hell?"

"I did it because I liked you."

"Fine way of showing it."

"I was a twelve year-old kid, Georgie. I told you I was sorry about your cat."

"Too late for *sorries*."

"Listen, we're in here together whether you like it or not. Let's just leave the past behind us and at least *try* to get along."

"Fine."

"You mind if I share my coat with you? It's getting cold in here."

Shaking, she extended one side of my wool coat. I slid beneath it drew close.

The darkness inside of that place was thick as one of my grandmother's wool sweaters. I couldn't see my own hand in front of my face. It was disorienting. The air was thin like at the top of a mountain in high altitude and the door was sealed.

I did see a crack in the ceiling, however and wondered if I could force the hatch in the roof open and climb out. I was going to need Georgie's help.

"You see that crack in the ceiling?"

I couldn't' see her, but I could hear her movements. In the short time I had been in the shed sitting in the dark, my hearing had become more acute.

She looked up. "Yeah, I see it."

"I can't get up there by myself. I need your help."

She shook her head.

I clicked the light on my digital watch and tried to see her face.

"I can't move."

"Why?"

"I think I'm frostbitten. I can't walk," she cried.

We'd sat in the darkness for forty five minutes by then.

"If you want to get out of here you'll have to try. Got it?"

I stood and tried to pull her with me but her legs collapsed under her from the cold. Her hands were stiff and frozen. She couldn't move. She couldn't even hold my hand.

"Shit, Georgie."

I knew we were in trouble then.

It looked like stage 3 hypothermia. I learned about it on a mountain climbing expedition after high school. I didn't want Georgie to die on me so I told her to stay under my coat as I used the light from my watch to find my way to the other side of the room. I couldn't' find a ladder, a chair, or anything to help me climb to the roof. But I did find a thick burlap covering.

I made my way back to Georgie and wrapped us in the burlap cover. I spared as much body heat as I could, burying us under my coat and anything I could pile on top of us. Then I prayed for Georgie's life...and mine.

****

There was a look of disbelief in Louis Louvelle's eyes as he listened to Jake's story.
"But that's not all that happened between you and my daughter," he said.

Jake met the man's cold hard stare. "I won't to lie to you."

****

"...Georgie?"

"Yes?"

"You still here?"

"Barely..." she groaned.

"What's the first thing you want when we get out of here?"

"Fresh baked apple fritters," she laughed.
It probably wasn't Stage 3 hypothermia yet. She was still alert and had even managed to tell a joke.

"I can't get to the roof. But our cars are parked on the side of the road. Somebody will find us...*eventually*."

I rubbed her arms to generate heat.

"We need to get your blood circulating. Care for a walk around the room?"

"I can't. My feet are numb. I can't feel them anymore."

We were there an hour and a half. My toes were starting to get numb too. We huddled under the burlap covering, our legs entwined, breathing each other's air.

"Thanks for coming to my rescue," she said in a somber voice. "You wouldn't be in this situation if it wasn't for me."

"You're right," I smiled. "I would have waited next to our cars if it was some other girl."

"Why?"

"Because I love you," I answered in a serious tone.

"Yeah right. What you felt for me was just a silly childhood crush," she laughed. "You don't love me..."

"I risked my life to be here with you. If that's not love, I don't know what is."

"I haven't seen you in seven years! You can't possibly be in love with me."

I closed my eyes and tried not to notice the soft sweet smell of her hair. My intentions were honorable. But soon, the heat our bodies generated together petered out. Would we make it out of there alive? Would she ever know the truth?

I looked at my digital watch again, using its light to illuminate her face. Georgie had fallen asleep. We were there for roughly two and a half hours when she pressed her head against my chest, draining my body heat like a vampire draining blood.

Not even the burlap cover I found nearby could keep us warm much longer.

I was shaking and my fingers were starting to get numb while Georgie trembled beside me. Her beautiful face lay frozen like a Popsicle. We had to do something.

****

Louis stood arm's distance from Jake's face, breathing sharply. But the young man refused to finish his story out of respect for his wife and her father.

****

"You feel like a block of ice," Georgie said, teeth chattering.

"You too," I answered.

"What are we going to do?"

"Even my blood is cold. We can't hide under this burlap blanket all night. We have to at *least try* to get out."

"But I can't stand," she answered, voice quivering.

I laid my head against hers.

"Maybe if you jogged around, you'll work up the strength again?" she suggested.

"My legs are too numb. But don't worry Georgie, I'll get us out of here."

"How?"

I could hear the fear in her voice. The panic. I moved to sit up, drew the blankets away and look around the shed again, but she pulled me back.

"You feel that blast of cold air? You're gonna kill yourself."

"At least I died trying."

Georgie snapped the burlap blanket closed and held my hand. "Don't leave…"

I settled beside her, her nose brushing against mine. We kissed and soon, one thing led to another.

A short time later, blood was flowing warm in our veins again. But in the end it wasn't enough. I realize now that what we did together was probably the worst thing we could do. Our pores cooled rapidly making us even more susceptible to the cold air. Not to mention the amount of oxygen we depleted with our activities in such a limited amount of air. We were there another hour, frozen with hypothermia and on the brink of death. The road was all but deserted in the middle of the night. I drove it often. I knew no one would find us until morning and by then it would be too late.

Time seemed to pass very slowly. Georgie had stopped talking, falling into a deep sleep. Or worse, a coma. I shook her but she was unresponsive. So I panicked.

I got up with the little mobility I had left and used the fading light on my watch to find my way around the shed again. I stumbled to the other side, which had gone unexplored and bumped into something frozen and cold. It felt like flesh so I screamed in terror, thinking I'd stumbled into a dead body. But it was only a carcass. The carcass of a dead cow.

I backed into another as I tried to move away. Then I counted. There were other slabs of meat and frozen deer. Dozens of them.

Suddenly, I had an idea. I dragged some of the cow carcasses across the room one by one and piled them as high as I could. My heart was racing. I knew the circulation in my blood was slowing and all of it was pumping into my heart. Which could kill me. But strangely, the adrenalin kept me going.

I watched the whole pile topple and had to start all over again with frost bit fingers until I finally had enough to climb to the top and push a hatch in the roof open.

With one triumphant life defining moment I jumped and caught the edge of the crack. I pushed the roof open and pulled myself out. But all I could think about was Georgie. I didn't know if she was dead or not. I just had to get her out.

I took a breath of fresh warm air, by comparison, the inside of that shed was icier than it was outside! I was so happy to be standing there, so happy to be alive. For the first time in my life the stars never looked more beautiful and the moon never looked so bright.

I stood on the roof and looked at the ground below at little patches of dead grass and snow. There wasn't a safe place to land or a place to climb down and suddenly I was sliding on thin ice. I jumped. When I landed I heard a loud crack. I knew my leg was broken but that didn't stop me from trying to get Georgie out.

This time I was going to be careful. I limped across the field and found a big piece of log. I dragged it to the shed. Then I pushed the bolt back and made sure the log was secure before I went in.

I was terrified. I thought the door was going to close and lock us in again. I couldn't climb the mountain of carcasses with my broken leg.

Georgie was unconscious when I dragged

her out. I laid her on the ground and collapsed beside her. I must have bawled my eyes out. But I knew I couldn't lay there and cry for long. I had to get Georgie the medical attention she needed and quickly. I limped across the ditch to my car. Luckily, the local sheriff found our cars, and was already at the scene. When the ambulance arrived I was unconscious in the front seat of my car. But luckily I had already told the officer enough to find Georgie.

Turns out, we were locked in a *storage freezer* for nearly four hours. It was a miracle we lasted that long.

****

"So that's the story? The real story? In the settlement you signed an agreement vowing to stay away from my daughter. She was seventeen years-old, Jake. Why come back?"

"I never wanted to leave in the first place. You wouldn't let me see her."

"I had my reasons."

"I risked life and limb for your daughter and you sued me."

Jake's chest heaved up and down in anger.

"Enjoying your retirement? The land you paid for with my family's money? You all but accused me of rape. You forced my family into an embarrassing situation for your own gain."

"I did it to protect my daughter."

"I spent two weeks in the hospital and a month with my leg in a cast. I nearly died trying to save Georgie. How in the hell could anybody think I would do something to hurt her?"

"You did. And that's why I kept her away from you."

Jake took several deep restraining breaths inches away from Louis' face. He searched his eyes.

"But I have her now and there's nothing you can do about it."

Louis gave him an incredulous look. "And that's why you married her. You wanted revenge…"

Jake smirked.

"I tracked Georgie down and married her because I love her. Revenge simply sweetened the deal."

"What can I do to keep you away from my daughter? You want me to retract everything I said about you in my lawsuit? Pay the settlement back? What *do you* want?"

"I want Georgie... and now I have her. It didn't take much to do it. I just had to get her away from you."

"Get her away from me?"

Jake smiled at the ingenuity of his own plan. He tossed a fallen apple into a nearby barrel.

"Georgie didn't meet Lucky by accident. I hired him."

Louis looked like he wanted to strike him. He rubbed a hand across the top of his bald head. "I warned her..." he grumbled.

"What I didn't predict was that she'd actually fall for someone else. Good thing I got there when I did."

He turned a mocking glare onto his father-in-law.

"Your days of controlling and manipulating Georgie are over. She's mine."

"And what you did wasn't manipulative or controlling? She's got enough problems. The difference between the two of us is that I love my daughter."

"I love her too."

"I'm warning you Jake. Hurt my daughter, and I will kill you."

"Go ahead and try old man."

Jake grabbed an apple from one of the trees and bit it. He munched the fruit like he didn't have a care in the world as juice spilled from the corner of his mouth down his chin. He wiped it with the back of his hand.

The sound of leaves and grass rustling under foot made them turn around. Georgie had appeared on the trail and was walking straight toward them.

Jake smiled at Louis. "You gonna tell her the truth or shall I?"

"Don't go dredging up those old memories. She's been through enough! You bastard. You goddamn son-of-a-bitch!" Louis growled.

Jake bit the apple again and smiled as Georgie walked to him and gave him a hug. He kissed her on the lips.

"Is everything okay? I feel like I interrupted a showdown."

Jake smirked at Louis from over her shoulder.

"Sorry we took so long. Louis and I are almost done. Can you give us a few minutes, babe?"

Georgie smiled at her father. "Okay guys. But don't keep me waiting too long."

She spun on her heels and walked toward the field.

"Do you have a conscience?" Louis asked.

Jake took another bite of his apple.

"Have you any decency *at all*?"

Jake chomped the fruit in his mouth.

"You breached the agreement in our settlement. Therefore, I have the right to release our court documents to the press."

Jake swallowed the bite of apple and tossed the core.

"Go right ahead."

"You're bluffing."

"I was only nineteen years-old. My parents forced me to accept the terms of your agreement to keep you quiet."

"They had their reasons too."

"They were embarrassed. After all, you insinuated that I led your daughter to that shed and assaulted her. And they believed you," Jake sneered.

It was Louis' turned to smile.

"Like I said, I had my reasons."

"And I have mine. Of course, if you release our court records to the press people will form their own opinion about Georgie and her greedy parents. In fact, they'll think she's a gold digging whore out to get more money because *she married her alleged attacker*."

"Georgie knew nothing about the lawsuit or settlement and I prefer to keep it that way."

"Then I suggest you keep your silly court documents to yourself. Otherwise, I'll hire the best PR people in the world and come out of this smelling like a rose... How bad will you look?"

"You're a mean bastard."

"I learned from the best."

"So you're going to ruin Georgie's life?"

"The way you tried to ruin mine? Of course not. I'm not that evil. But I am the best thing that ever happened to Georgie. I'll give her everything you couldn't and more."

"Why?"

"I already told you. I love her."

When Jake set out to meet Georgie in Paris he went with revenge hot on his mind until he realized the woman he set out to ruin had no recollection of their past. She was beautiful, charming, talented, and sweet. And when they kissed in the VIP room that first night, he was in love all over again... not that he ever gave her up to begin with.

"Georgie's fragile. She doesn't deserve whatever plot you've hatched in your sick mind."

"Fragile? You have no idea what kind of daughter you have, do you? She's a strong confident woman fully capable of making her own decisions."

"And I guess you're living proof."

"Don't talk like that about her."

"Did you ever wonder why Georgie didn't remember you in France?"

"It's been eleven years. I look a little different, so does she."

Louis drew close to Jake's face. "But no memory of you at all? The fact that she couldn't remember seeing her cat get hit by a car?"

Jake waited for Louis to finish, wondering where the man was leading him.

"A long time ago Georgie was the youngest cast member of one of the most popular TV shows in the country. But we pulled her out."

"What does that have to do with anything?"

"The reason she doesn't remember what happened between you that night…."

Louis took a deep breath and turned his back to Jake.

"Will you spit it out already?"

"Georgie was abducted when she was six years-old. She was gone three days… Detectives took her for dead."

"She never told me…"

"Because she doesn't remember."

Jake's heart was racing. If he knew who the kidnapper was he'd kill him himself.

"Just like she blocked out the night we spent in the freezer."

"The night we rescued her, Georgie had already tried to escape but fell down a flight of stairs. She suffered a head injury which caused massive brain trauma in the area of her brain where memories are stored. As a result she has a rare stress induced form of Anterograde amnesia, which means Georgie's ability to make new memories in high stress situations is impaired. When she awoke from her hypothermia induced coma, she didn't remember anything at all.

"Who did this to her?"

"Some nutcase from the production company. A man named Curt Owens....luckily, footage from a running camera caught images of them leaving the set together."

Jake made a note to remember the man's name. He rubbed a hand over his face and shook his head. "I'm sorry…"

It made sense to him now, why Georgie didn't remember him. Time stood still for him in the years they'd been apart. It was mind boggling that she didn't remember him or their night together.

Jake suddenly felt ashamed for taunting his father-in-law. He seemed like a decent guy. Anger made people do strange things and Jake was no exception to revenge or anger.

205 Infatuation by E. Hughes

"Now you understand why I'm so protective of my daughter. She's fragile, Jake. We have to be careful... there are a lot of issues, but we're slowly working on them."

"Then I'll get her the help she needs."

"Georgie's mother and I feel she's better off as long as she doesn't remember."

"I disagree. The longer a secret like that is repressed the more damage it causes."

"The memories aren't repressed, her brain never stored them. The man who kidnapped Georgie shot himself before officers could arrest him. I'm sorry I took you to court, son. At the time, all I could think about was Curt Owens and Georgie was suffering all over again. I was determined not to let anyone else get away with hurting my daughter."

"Maybe if you listened to my side story...."

"People don't think rationally when they're in pain. At first, we didn't know about the rest until she came to us two months later and..."

"And what?"

"She said something happened... her

mother and I had her examined and, we knew. I was angry, Jake. Our beautiful, seventeen year-old daughter."

"So where do we go from here Louis? Georgie and I are married. We love each other. I'm not going anywhere. You can't keep us apart anymore...."

"I know."

Louis walked to the trail with a brave face and looked over his shoulder at Jake.

"She's a woman now... so I guess we have to accept it."

"That's it?"

"Take good care of her."

Louis continued to the house. The door opened and Georgie came out. She started down the stairs toward the apple trees. Jake waited until her father was inside then jogged across the field to the house. She met him halfway.

"That must have been some talk!"

Jake swept Georgie into his arms and held her tight. She opened her mouth to speak but saw the staid expression on his face and decided to keep quiet.

They stood beneath a gold painted sky in

knee-high wheat colored grass that billowed back and forth between them as a gentle summer breeze blew across their faces.

The air was sweet, her mother's Rose bushes nearby. He looked at Georgie for the very first time and saw beyond her beauty, her talent, beyond her father's lies and misapprehensions, beyond his lust for revenge and saw a woman he truly loved and cared about. He let her go and looked up. Irma and Anne were on the porch and Olivia and Oliver were standing by the car.

"I talked to my mother. Olivia and Oliver are going with us," Georgie said.

"For how long?"

"A few weeks. Longer if we want."

He wasn't sure that he was ready to share Georgie just yet. They were only newly married. Georgie leaned forward and kissed Olivia on the head. It was uncanny how much the two of them looked alike.

Jake looked at Olivia and Oscar again and suddenly the past, present, and future converged and exploded into sharp realization.

Louis' anger suddenly made sense.

"--How old are the twins?" he asked.

"They're ten. Why?"

Jake grabbed Georgie's arm and led her away from the porch.

"What's wrong?" she asked, trying to keep pace.

"Your father and I were talking."

"I know. Is something wrong?"

Jake stopped when they were a safe distance away from the house.

"Georgie, he didn't tell me everything I needed to know, did he?"

"What did he tell you?"

"He told me about Cty Pd."

Georgie pulled her arm away.

"We don't talk about that."

Jake looked over his shoulder, trying not to draw attention to himself as he gripped her arms again.

"Listen to me, Georgie... we need to get everything out in the open," he whispered.

"Get what in the open! I told you we don't talk about that."

"I know the story."

"Why did he tell you?"

She turned and started angrily toward the

house where her father had gone inside.

"He didn't tell me anything. I know Because I was there."

Georgie came to a halt then spun around.

"What do you mean?"

"Promise you'll forgive me for what I'm about to tell you."

"Jake? You're freaking me out—"

He looked over his shoulder at the house. Irma and Anna were still waiting for them on the porch.

"I've been lying to you, G. We didn't meet at the Pink Poodle by accident. I went there to meet you."

"How is that possible? Why?"

"I wanted to see you again."

"What do you mean, 'see me again?' I feel like I'm in the Twilight Zone." Georgie looked helplessly over his shoulder at the house. "I feel like I don't know you right now. Why are you acting so crazy?"

"I'm not crazy and I didn't do anything wrong," Jake answered.

"You lied. How's that?"

"I lied because of your father."

"What does Louis have to do with any of

this?"

"I was locked in the storage shed on Cty Pd with you that night."

He waited for Georgie to hit him, run, scream... do something! But she simply stared at him with a blank face.

"How is that possible? I thought... someone from the party followed me off-road? That was you?"

"No—I didn't follow you from a party. I saw your car on the side of the road. I tried to help you. Don't you remember?"

"I don't remember anything."

"Your father told me you suffer from a rare form of stress induced anterograde amnesia."

"So—what does this mean?" she asked, eyes on the brink of tears.

He could only imagine what her father had led her to believe all those years. Jake sank to his knees and pulled Georgie's hand into his.

"Georgie, please, I would never-ever do anything to hurt you. I was just trying to help. I was driving home one night and saw your car on the side of the road. I wanted to help you."

"How did you know it was my car? We didn't even know each other!"

"We went to All Savior's together. You remember Paul Cutter-- why can't you *remember me*?"

She shook her head. "What does Paul have to do with anything? I don't remember you, Jake."

"You'd have to remember the kid you accused of killing your cat."

Georgie gasped then an old look of childhood disgust crossed her face.

"You're Jughead? I can't believe you! Oh my dear lord, this is the worst thing you have ever done. So everything in France and Italy was just one of your cruel pranks."

Jake leapt to his feet as she crumpled her hand and swung. Her fist landed against his chest with a thud. He grabbed her arms.

"I'm not the same guy anymore, Georgie.

Can't you forgive the past? We were kids for fuck's sake."

"It's not about being kids anymore. It's about the lies, Jake. You lied when you met me, you lied to get me to go Italy with you!

You had that wedding planned the whole time. It was just a cruel elaborate joke to you, wasn't it? Just another childhood bully who never grew up! Chris told me but I didn't believe him because I trusted you! You didn't tell the truth about anything and now that you know about Cty Pd and what happened to me in that storage shed, you're twisting the knife to hurt me even more. Why are you making this up? Why are you doing this to me?"

"I'm not trying to hurt you, G. Did you think you could hide the truth forever? Yes—I was a spoiled asshole and bully when we were kids. Yes, I lied when we were in France and didn't tell you about our past. But I'm not lying about the shed. Your father can vouch for me, Georgie. After all, he took me to court. He accused me of rape. Is that what you think? That I raped you in the storage shed?"

He gave her a helpless look.

"I don't remember what happened in the storage shed!"

"Well let me assure you, Georgie that it wasn't rape! I have lived with your father's lie for eleven years. How do you think that makes me feel? I have loved you since we were kids. For you to think I would do something like this to you kills me. That you can stand there and look at me like that, or even think I was capable of doing such an evil thing to anyone, *especially* you...."

"Then what were you doing in the shed?"

"I saw your car on the side of the road. I parked in front of you because I thought you were in danger. We had an argument and you ran to the shed and locked yourself in. I opened the shed to get you out but the door bolted shut behind me and locked me in. We were locked inside for hours. You told me you wanted Apple Fritters when you got out. I never gave them to you. Your father wouldn't let me see you. I tried, Georgie but there was a restraining order. So the first thing I did when I visited you in France was made good on my promise. Look at me Georgie, I would never do anything to hurt you."

"I don't understand... I was so young... Why would I do something like that—"

"We liked each other and were just trying

to keep warm," Jake shrugged.

He met her eyes.

"If you don't believe me we can hire a therapist—a hypnotist, someone to help you remember. I want you to remember...I found you because I love you and needed you to vindicate me from your father's lies."

He wasn't ready to accept the possibility that Georgie could never remember what they shared. Their memories had to be hidden somewhere inside of that head of hers.

"But I don't remember! I'm still trying to piece everything together.... and it's starting to make sense...Jake, my father was so angry when he saw us together. He knew it was you the entire time. He's been keeping us apart. He's been lying to me about that night for eleven years...."

"A few months after the Cty Pd incident, Louis filed a wrongful injury lawsuit. In the paperwork he claimed I lured his daughter into a storage shed and was responsible for your injuries. He also said that you were assaulted and while you didn't remember the crime, there was DNA evidence to link me to it. I told him something happened in the shed but it was consensual. Louis got angry and threatened to file criminal charges so my parents settled. They died, thinking their only son was a sociopath. I endured years of humiliating therapy. No one believed my side of the story."

Georgie shook her head, eyes welling with tears.

"I'm sorry my father did that to you. He told us he didn't know who the other person in the shed was and that we were moving to Cornwall to get away. My mother didn't know where he got the money to buy land or the house from so it all makes sense…"

"Your family moved to Cornwall to hide you, didn't they?"

Georgie buried her face in her hands and cried.

"Your father said you came to him a few months later--"

Georgie shut her eyes. "It was difficult. But I love Olivia and Oliver, we all do. I'm sorry I didn't tell you about them in France."

"I would have been there for you. Thank God I didn't give up or we would never have known the truth."

Jake went into his pocket and gave Georgie a handkerchief. She wiped her eyes and the mascara running down her cheeks.

"My father's not evil. He was just trying to protect me."

"I would do anything to protect my daughter too, so I can't blame him for being cruel to the kid who got his daughter pregnant."

Jake sighed and took a deep breath.

"I'm so sorry—for everything. I don't what you're feeling right now."

"I'm still in shock. I'm confused. I'm angry…."

"Tell me how to make it better. I'll do anything…."

"I want you to tell me exactly what happened in the shed that night."

"I don't want to."

"Why?"

"I want you to remember on your own…"

There was always hope.

"What if I can't?"

"As long as you still love me it doesn't matter… *I love you, G.* Do you love me? Or is that done and over with now?"

The look on Georgie's face softened.

"When did I ever say I didn't love you anymore, huh Jughead?" she nudged his arm and smiled.

Jake grimaced.

"Promise you will never call me by that name again." He wrapped an arm around Georgie's shoulder and led her across the field toward the house. Through tears, she was smiling that beautiful smile of hers.

"Why not? I think I can get used to calling you that. Maybe get revenge for the hell you put me through when we were kids. You were terrible!"

He remembered how much she hated him and laughed.

"Get all the revenge you want. You're a cruel woman, Georgine **Lyggle** -- *I think I can get used to calling you that!*"

"It's good. I like it."

"Well, the good news is that you get to keep it. The bad news is that you're stuck with me."

They walked hand in hand back to the house to Irma and Anne's exasperated faces.

Irma was the first to come downstairs and give Jake a hug.

"Jeez. What's going on with you two?"

Georgie stole a peek at Irma. "Jake and I had a heart-to-heart. We still have a lot to discuss so I'll tell you about it later, mama."

Anne followed Irma and gave her sister and her new brother-in-law a hug. "Welcome to the family, Jake. Hope dad wasn't too rough on ya. I think he's coming around."

Irma gave the kids a suitcase and two bags with their clothes and extra blankets inside.

Jake stared at Olivia and Oliver as they climbed into the back seat.

"Absolutely. Welcome to the family, Jake. We're glad to have you. Just take good care of my Georgine," Irma said.

Jake kissed her on the cheek. "I will."

Louis watched from his bedroom window as Jake and Georgie climbed into the car and drove away. Irma and Anne waved goodbye from the porch until the car was out of sight, blazing down a dusty country road....

THE END.